BEN YOKOYAMA
AND THE COOKIE OF
PERFECTION

THE COOKIE CHRONICLES

Cookie Chronicles BOOK THREE

BEN YOKOYAMA AND THE COOKIE OF PERFECTION

BY
MATTHEW SWANSON
&
ROBBI BEHR

ALFRED A. KNOPF
NEW YORK

THIS IS A BORZOI BOOK PUBLISHED BY ALFRED A. KNOPF

Visit us on the Web! rhcbooks.com

Educators and librarians, for a variety of teaching tools, visit us at RHTeachersLibrarians.com

Library of Congress Cataloging-in-Publication Data is available upon request.
ISBN 978-0-593-30277-4 (trade) — ISBN 978-0-593-12690-5 (lib. bdg.) — ISBN 978-0-593-12691-2 (ebook)

The text of this book is set in 14-point Bembo.
The illustrations were created using Adobe Photoshop, combining digital linework with hand-painted watercolor washes.
Interior design by Robbi Behr

Printed in the United States of America
December 2021
10 9 8 7 6 5 4 3 2 1

First Edition

For Dorothea Ziegler,
teacher of piano and
maker of moonlight

CHAPTER 1

Ben Yokoyama had a pretty good life.

He lived with his mom and his dad in a house that had three ceiling fans, a garbage disposal, and a roof that didn't leak when it rained.

He had a dog named Dumbles, who would sometimes fetch a tennis ball and often gave cuddles and licks.

His best friend, Janet, lived in the house just behind his. She had a trampoline, a comfortable blue chair, and a pantry that usually contained marshmallows.

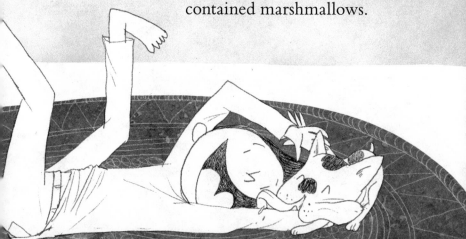

Ben had nothing to complain about, so he usually didn't complain. But some days, he had to.

Because some days, his mom burned the pancakes.

 Sorry, Ben! said Ben's mom, setting a plateful of scorched, food-like slabs on the table.

They're a little bit crispy.

It was not an accurate description.

Potato chips were crispy.

Fried chicken was crispy.

The pancakes were a charbroiled insult wrapped in a smoldering lie.

"That's okay," said Ben the way someone might say,

What's that awful smell?

when a wet goat walks into the room.

 WHAT...?

"Look," said Ben's mom, bending down and offering Dumbles a pancake. "Dumby likes them."

Dumbles took one sniff of the not-a-pancake and fled into the living room.

"Good boy," said Ben's dad, who had once read in a magazine that it was unhealthy for dogs to eat human food.

"How about you, Ken?" asked Ben's mom.

"You know . . . I just remembered that we're having a *special* breakfast at work today. Martha is bringing muffins."

"But you don't *like* muffins."

"Maybe today is the day I finally will! I always tell *Ben* to keep an open mind."

Ben's dad was a terrible liar. Saying anything but the truth made him sweaty and cross-eyed.

Ben's mom made a face that said, *I wish you could see how sweaty and cross-eyed you look.*

3

"I could have . . . maybe just . . . *one* of these pancakes without ruining my appetite," Ben's dad offered.

"It would be my *pleasure* to serve you one," said Ben's mom, placing three singed wafers of unparalleled sadness on his plate.

Usually Ben's dad made breakfast. And dinner. And lunch on the weekends. Because he was just so much better at cooking. For her part, Ben's mom changed the oil in the car and used the chainsaw to lop off suspicious-looking tree limbs.

But Ben's mom was trying to learn how to cook, so they had started *Monday Meals with Mom!* The idea had seemed so great before the actual cooking began.

Ben had even made a sign. He now regretted the exclamation point.

Ben's dad picked up his fork and knife and cut a bite so small it wouldn't have made a hungry hamster happy.

"I guess the rest of these *delicious* pancakes are all for you, Ben," said his mom, sliding six discs of blackened apocalypse onto his plate.

Ben panicked. It was a family rule that you had to eat *everything* on your plate, whether you liked it or not.

He reached down into the center of his misery and came back with an idea.

> What about *you*, Mom? It wouldn't be right to take all these pancakes for myself. I insist you have at least four.

"I'm on a diet," she snapped.

"You *are*?" This was news to Ben. He had seen her eat a full rack of ribs the night before.

"But *why*?" asked Ben's dad.

HEALTH, said Ben's mom with the frosty resolve of a snowcapped Himalaya.

Ben's mom was an *excellent* liar. Ben looked at his dad. His dad looked at Ben. They both looked at Ben's mom wide-eyed, like someone who has just read the first chapter of a thrilling mystery and is desperate to know how it ends.

"Nora is on a special diet where she eats nothing but ground beef and bananas," Ben's mom continued. "I've decided to try it."

Nora was Ben's aunt. Ben liked Nora a lot, but Ben's mom usually rolled her eyes at the things Nora did, said, wore, and ate. Never in her whole life had Ben's mom done something just because Aunt Nora did.

"Well, why don't you grab a banana and join us?" Ben's dad suggested, patting the place mat beside him.

But the fruit bowl was empty.

I ate my bananas before you guys got up,

said Ben's mom with a look that was ever-so-slightly cross-eyed.

That's strange. I didn't see any peels when I emptied the trash can earlier.

I also ate the peels,

said Ben's mom, looking somewhat sweaty now, too.

Ben was starting to wonder if maybe his mom wasn't such an excellent liar after all.

"That's an *interesting* diet," said Ben. It seemed impossible that eating banana peels was a good idea in any universe. He couldn't wait to ask Nora if it was true.

"Oh yes. It's quite something," said Ben's mom. "Now, please, my men. Enjoy your meal."

But asking Ben to enjoy the pancakes was like asking a snowman to enjoy a cup of hot chocolate. He searched the distant corners of his mind for a way to get around the problem.

He could dump his pancakes on the floor and hope that no one noticed. He could run out the door and never come back. Or . . .

Ben had a better idea. A simpler one. He looked down at his watch and very much liked what he saw.

Oh *shucks*, would you look at the time? I really *must* be going,

he said, standing up and carrying his plate across the room in one fluid motion.

If I don't leave now, I might be late to meet Janet at the corner. And you know how I feel about being late.

We sure do,

said Ben's dad, like one wobbling bowling pin says to another.

Don't we, Linda?

I am familiar with your legendary punctuality,

said Ben's mom, like the ball as it races down the lane.

I'm *just so sorry* that I don't have time to finish my *delicious* pancakes,

said Ben as he placed his untouched plateful of crunchy despair in the sink. Ben was a better liar than his dad but not nearly as good as his mom.

He grabbed his coat and his backpack and was halfway out the door when his dad said, "Wait!"

Ben thought about making a break for it. One more step and he'd be free of the horrible pancakes forever.

"Your jersey!" his dad continued.

Suddenly Ben remembered. He had asked his dad to wash his jersey so he could wear it to school.

"Thanks," said Ben, taking the jersey. He was about to put it on when he noticed something.

What . . . *happened?*

It wasn't an actual question, because the answer didn't really matter. What mattered was the endless mess of greasy blotches all over his jersey.

Oh, Ken,

said Ben's mom.

Well, shucks, said Ben's dad without further explanation. Because no further explanation was needed. Ben and his mom knew this story pretty well.

Sometimes, or maybe even often, Ben's dad left tubes of lip balm in the pocket of his pants when he put them in the laundry, which meant they melted in the dryer and left great greasy blotches all over the clothes.

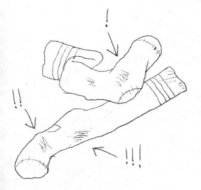

Ben was only halfway mad when his socks got greasy or his *Ski Minnesota!* sweatshirt got blotchy, but his jersey was *different*.

It was the jersey of first baseman Pete (The Big) Bubango of the Honeycutt Melons. *The Big Bubango had signed it himself!*

"I'm so sorry," said Ben's dad.

Ben was speechless. "Sorry" was for when you accidentally bumped into someone in the cafeteria and made them spill their milk a little.

This was a moment for shouting forbidden words as sky-splitting lightning sets nearby trees on fire.

His once-in-a-lifetime jersey was ruined.

"Maybe I can get it out with that special spray I bought for grass stains," said Ben's mom with her *All is not lost* face.

"I thought that spray didn't really work," said Ben's dad with his *Of course I hope it works, but I don't want to get Ben's hopes up* face.

"It didn't work for jeans. But maybe it *will* work for Ben's jersey," said Ben's mom with her *Hope is not a strategy* face.

Ben looked at his watch. If he didn't leave right away, he actually *would* be late.

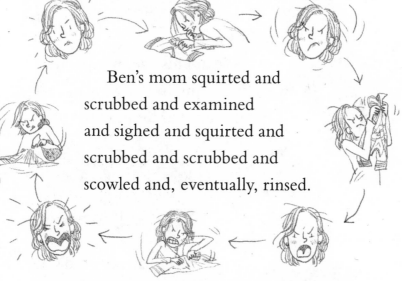

Ben's mom squirted and scrubbed and examined and sighed and squirted and scrubbed and scrubbed and scowled and, eventually, rinsed.

Ben's heart hoped for a clean jersey the way someone hopes for sunshine on the morning of his outdoor birthday party.

"Hmm," said Ben's mom, handing the jersey to Ben. It wasn't an encouraging sound. "I think it looks *much* better now."

Ben did not agree. The jersey was just as greasy as it had been before. But now it was also damp. Ben scowled like someone whose birthday party has just been canceled due to hail.

"It will look better when it dries," said Ben's mom unconvincingly.

Ben took off his shirt and put on his jersey instead. He felt hungry, greasy, wet, and cold.

Some days just don't start out the way you want them to,

said his dad, putting his arms around Ben and pulling him in for a hug.

But it doesn't mean they have to *end* that way. You never know what today might bring.

Usually his dad's pep talks did the trick, but today Ben didn't *want* to be cheered up.

He flew out the door and raced to the corner with the yellow bush, determined to get there on time.

While Ben sprinted his way along the sidewalk, he thought about the things he wanted.

Pancakes that weren't burnt.

A clean, dry jersey.

And to get to the corner on time.

It didn't seem like a lot to ask.

Ben looked at his watch and ran faster. He got there with seventeen seconds to spare.

Then he waited.

And waited.

Because Janet was late.

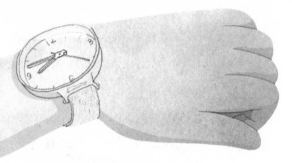

CHAPTER 2

Janet was often late.

Most mornings, Ben didn't mind. Because waiting meant time to make up limericks or search for four-leaf clovers. But today he was already halfway mad, and the waiting made him madder.

Two minutes passed. Then seven. Then thirteen.

Eventually, Janet showed up.

"Good morning," she said with a smile.

Ben looked away. Janet's smile had a way of warming him up, and he wanted to stay chilly for a while. He started marching down the sidewalk toward the school.

Janet scurried to keep up.

What's your deal? she asked, trying to catch her breath.

You're late.

Janet looked at her watch and shrugged.

I'm exactly as late as I was on Friday.

Exactly, said Ben. As far as he was concerned, Janet was making his point for him.

Friday you didn't stomp away the second I showed up.

That was true. But on Friday Ben hadn't been hungry and grease-stained and wet. He knew that Janet was only partly responsible for his bad mood. But he wanted her to take the whole blame.

Ben marched on in a hurried huff.

"Sheesh," said Janet with breathless exasperation. "Would you hold on a second? I have something for you."

That got Ben's attention. Getting something was better than being mad. He took a deep breath and told the angry part of him to take a five-minute time-out.

"What is it?"

"Mom and I went to the Chinese restaurant last night. I saved my fortune cookie for you."

"Oh," said Ben, trying to seem less excited than he actually was.

Thanks.

Janet smiled. She knew that Ben's two soft spots were delicious desserts and wise words. Fortune cookies had *both*.

Ben cracked open the cookie and read the fortune.

Practice makes perfect.

The wisdom hit Ben like the sunrise hits the early-morning shadows. Suddenly everything was perfectly clear!

It *wasn't* that his parents were hopeless.

Janet *wasn't* a lost cause.

It was *entirely possible* that all three of them might *eventually* be perfect.

They just had some practicing to do.

CHAPTER 3

Ben got to school and sat down at his desk. When the bell rang, his teacher, Mr. Piscarelli, stood at the front of the room and held up a sheet of paper.

Exciting news, folks. For the first time ever, someone got a perfect score on one of my math tests.

A chorus of gasps flared up like sudden fireworks. Whatever the *actual* math topic, Mr. P. always threw in one impossible problem. A problem with x's and y's and z's and unusual squiggles and fractions wobbling nervously on top of other fractions.

A problem that might have made an interesting decoration on the side of a lunch box but that no third grader could possibly solve. But someone *had*!

Everyone looked around, trying to figure out who it could possibly be. Ben thought it was probably Walter, who was extremely good with numbers, or Amy Lou Bonnerman, who always got all of the *other* questions on the math tests right. Or Janet, who was just plain smart in spite of never quite being on time.

Theories swirled around the room like a great flock of swallows looking for a good place to land.

Mr. P. waited for everyone to settle down.

"I'm pleased to announce that the person with the perfect score is . . . Darby Washington."

All at once, everyone turned toward the desk at the back of the room. It had sat empty until a few weeks before, when a new student had shown up one day with no warning.

For a few days, everyone had tried to figure out what Darby was all about and what kinds of tricks he could do. But he didn't say much and didn't seem to have any tricks. He usually spent recess watching other kids play kickball instead of joining in.

Ben hadn't given Darby much thought. Because even though Ben would never have said it out loud, Darby seemed a little . . . boring.

But getting a perfect score on an impossible math test was a *very* good trick.

"Congratulations, Darby," said Mr. P. "How is it that you happen to know calculus?" Mr. P. was using his *I'm just kidding around* voice, but Darby's face was deadly serious.

"Do you really want to know?"

"Of course," said Mr. P. "If you're willing to tell us."

Darby looked like he was trying to figure out how to coax an elephant through a keyhole.

Actually, I'd rather not say.

There was an awkward silence.

No . . . problem,

said Mr. P., giving Darby a curious look.

Keep up the good work!
I guess I'll have to make
my next test even *harder*.

I eagerly anticipate the challenge,

said Darby with a face like
he was going to a funeral.

Someone groaned. It was Kyle.

On one hand, Kyle was right. It was a
strange way for a third grader to talk.

But Ben smelled something
interesting. He wanted to know
how Darby had managed to do
the impossible.

He made up his mind. He
was going to find out.

CHAPTER 4

At recess, Ben went over to play kickball like he always did. He played for a few minutes before pretending he needed to tie his shoe and that the best place to tie it was on the bench where Darby was sitting.

Ben worked on his laces and waited for Darby to say something. But Darby just sat there, silently watching the kickball.

Eventually, Ben made the first move. "So . . . how did you do it?"

"What do you mean?" asked Darby, who seemed genuinely puzzled that someone was talking to him.

"I mean, that math problem was literally impossible to solve."

Darby bristled. "No problem is impossible . . . if you know how to solve it."

That halfway made sense, but Ben kept getting stuck on the half that didn't.

Right, but no one has ever gotten a perfect score on *any* of Mr. P.'s math tests . . . not *ever.* So how did *you?*

I happen to know a lot about calculus.

What is calculus, anyway?

It's the kind of math you use to figure out the derivatives and integrals of functions.

Ben was pretty sure Darby was speaking English. He had understood the words "math" and "figure," but the rest made about as much sense as a postcard from his grandma before his dad translated it from Japanese into English.

"It sounds complicated. How did you figure it out?"

"My dad taught me the basics. Then I read some books and did a bunch of practice tests until I understood the concepts perfectly."

That got Ben's attention. "*What* did you say?"

"I said, I read some books and—"

"No. The part at the end. Did you just say you're *perfect* at calculus?"

Darby hesitated. "I mean, no one's *perfect* at anything, right?"

But the words felt forced, like Darby was hiding a squirrel in his sweater and didn't want to admit it.

Ben leaned forward, excited and determined. "But . . . you chose the word 'perfect.' Why?"

Darby gave Ben a long, close look. "Why do you care so much?"

Ben pulled out his fortune and showed it to Darby, who read it carefully before handing it back with a nod.

"Let's just say," said Darby, as if he were dipping his toe in a pool to check the temperature before doing a cannonball, "it's been a long time since I met a calculus problem I didn't know how to tackle."

Ben's brain connected dots.

"So, you're admitting you're *perfect* at calculus?"

"I guess I am," said Darby, who seemed relieved. "It feels kind of good to say it out loud."

Ben was thrilled! He'd never met anyone who was perfect at anything. This was his golden opportunity to learn how to be perfect himself. But . . . he wasn't particularly interested in calculus. Which made him wonder, "Are you perfect at other things, too?"

Darby glanced around to see if anyone else was close enough to hear. And then he leaned over and whispered, "Can you keep a secret?"

"Of course."

"*Darby* isn't perfect. But . . ."

"*But what?*" Ben thought it was pretty weird that Darby had just referred to himself as "Darby," but he decided to let it go because he also sensed that something *big* was about to happen. Something that might change his life *forever.*

Tell me!

Ben grabbed the back of the bench to keep from floating away in sheer excitement.

It's better if I show you.

Darby took off his glasses

and slid them into his shirt pocket.

He straightened his back,

flipped up his collar,

and raised one eyebrow like a magician who knows he's about to amaze you.

31

Ben barely recognized the person beside him on the bench. It was still Darby, *sort of,* but everything was different. This person was taller and stronger and much more magnificent.

What just happened? Ben needed to know.

Pleased to meet you, Ben. I'm Darbino. I'm a little embarrassed to say it, but since you asked, I am . . .

Perfect?

Darbino winked.

You said it, not me.

Are you some kind of . . . ?

Superhero?

Ben nodded so hard he got a neck cramp.

I mean, it depends on your definition. I can't fly, for example.

Can you talk to animals or melt spoons with your mind?

I can't.

What *are* your powers?

Acrobatics,

kickball,

and, of course,

calculus.

Ben's mind went wild! But Darbino wasn't done.

Also, competitive cup stacking,

improbable courage,

and an uncommon tolerance for extremely spicy foods.

"But . . . ? How . . . ? What . . . ?" Ben had never talked to an actual superhero.

Darbino could tell he needed help. "Let's just say I'm kind of like Batman: a mortal human with surprising capabilities."

"Do you have gadgets?"

"Nope," said Darbino, resting his mighty hand on Ben's shoulder. "To be honest, I don't need them."

Ben shivered. Suddenly everything was different. All his dreams seemed to be coming true. He wanted to believe, but he needed to be *sure*. "Could you, maybe, do something . . . *super*?"

It would be my pleasure,

said Darbino, placing his feet together and bending ever so slightly at the knees. Then, in one thrilling motion, he leaped straight up and kicked his feet backward over his head, completing a full flip and landing effortlessly.

34

It was even more amazing than melting spoons with your mind.

Darbino made the tiniest of bows and sat back down on the bench.

Ben would have been speechless if he hadn't had so much to say. "I . . . can't believe you've just been sitting in the back of the classroom this whole time! I mean, you've always seemed so—" Ben swallowed the rest of his sentence.

You were going to say "boring."

I wasn't!

"It's okay," said Darbino. "Darby is quiet and shy and not very good at making friends. Darby doesn't even know how to play kickball."

"But you're . . . *perfect* at kickball?"

"You have no idea."

"Then why isn't Darby good at it, too?"

"Why don't you ask him yourself?" said Darbino, putting his glasses back on, smoothing down his collar, and slouching back into his old self.

"Darby?" said Ben.

"Yeah," said Darby. "It's me again."

Ben had a million questions. "What does Darbino like to eat? Have you *always* been Darbino? What is Darbino's tragic backstory?"

Ben assumed that Darby had been bitten by a radioactive scorpion or caught in a toxic rainstorm or abducted by aliens and injected with some sort of serum.

Darby spoke in a secretive whisper: "I'm afraid I can't talk about it here. *Anyone* could be listening."

Ben looked around. Darby had an excellent point. There were kids *everywhere*.

But there was one question Ben couldn't resist. "Whatever you did to become Darbino, can you do it to me?"

Darby gave Ben a look like a full-grown eagle gives a wet baby hatchling who just wriggled out of its shell. "I can't make you into a superhero, Ben. You either are or you aren't."

Ben wasn't surprised. But he was disappointed.

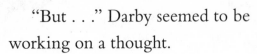

"But . . ." Darby seemed to be working on a thought.

"But?" Ben let himself feel a flicker of hope.

"Darbino *might* be able to give you some pointers."

Ben was excited! Ben was inspired! *Ben was extremely impatient!*

"When can we start?"

"Anytime, but . . ." Darby gave Ben a serious look. "Before we go any further, I have two conditions."

"Sure!"

First, you can't tell *anyone* about Darbino. *Ever*.

Why not?

Ben didn't understand. Being a superhero was *amazing*. He wasn't sure why Darby wasn't shouting about it from the top of a ladder.

"Because, as weird as it seems, most people don't actually like it when someone is perfect. Instead of being happy for me, it makes them feel worse about themselves."

Ben remembered Kyle's groan. Maybe Darby was right. "I definitely won't tell. And just so you know, I think it's amazing and wonderful."

"I'm glad you think so."

"What's the second condition?"

Darby looked out across the schoolyard and shook his head softly. "It's not easy being perfect. It requires a great deal of commitment."

"No problem," said Ben. "I practice piano every day for thirty minutes."

"That's a good start," said Darby. "But it also demands certain . . . *sacrifices*."

Ben was worried.

Ben was excited!

Ben was extremely confused.

Like what?

"I'm not sure how to say it. Hold on a second." Darby took off his glasses and popped up his collar, and suddenly Darbino was back, even more magnificent than before. It made Ben's eyes ache a little.

"Listen, Ben, if I'm going to teach you to be perfect, there's something you have to do for me."

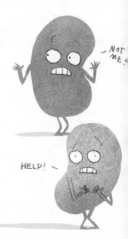

Ben had been waiting for the catch. Whenever something seemed too good to be true, it usually was. Would Darbino ask for his scooter or one of his kidneys? Or *both* of his kidneys?

"What do I have to do?"

"*Trust* me. I might ask you to do some unexpected things. But the road to perfection is not a straight line. I need you to believe in me, Ben. Because I can already tell I believe in you."

Ben got to keep his scooter! And both of his kidneys!

Having an open mind and taking advice
from a superhero was something he could do.

Is that it?

Yep. Does that work for you?

Yes!

Great. Then we have a deal.

They shook hands just
as the recess bell rang.

"To be continued," said Darby, putting
his glasses back on. "Can you come over
to my house after school?"

Ben thought about that. *Technically,* he was
supposed to walk home with Janet. *Technically,*
he needed a special note from his parents to walk
home with Darby instead.

But he had just been handed the chance of
a lifetime. If anyone complained, Ben would
simply explain that any rule he broke while
figuring out how to be perfect must be somehow
imperfect itself.

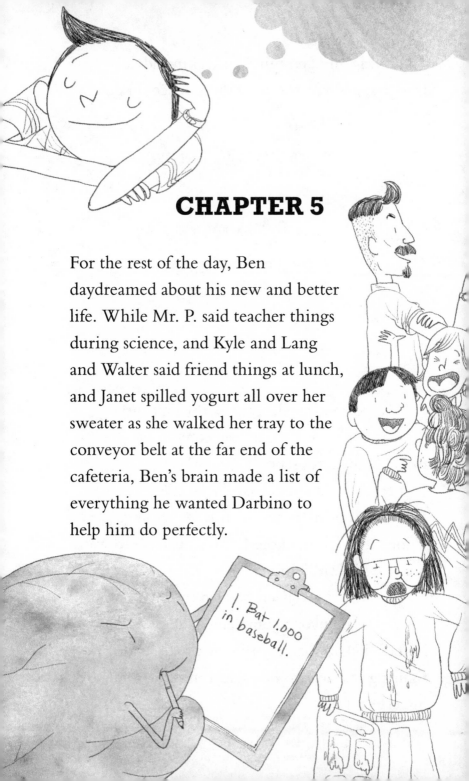

CHAPTER 5

For the rest of the day, Ben daydreamed about his new and better life. While Mr. P. said teacher things during science, and Kyle and Lang and Walter said friend things at lunch, and Janet spilled yogurt all over her sweater as she walked her tray to the conveyor belt at the far end of the cafeteria, Ben's brain made a list of everything he wanted Darbino to help him do perfectly.

1. Bat 1.000 in baseball.

Ben loved baseball. He loved waiting in
the outfield to see what would happen when
the pitcher threw the ball, knowing that,
at any second, he might have to make
a running catch or a leaping dive or
a sudden throw. Ben loved
playing defense.

The problem with baseball
was how hard it was to get a hit.

Kyle hit .400, which was best in the league. But it still meant that he got a hit only *four out of every ten times* he went to bat! Ben hit .200, which meant he got a hit only *two out of every ten times*!

"If our batting averages were grades on a math test, we'd both get an F!" Ben would often say after striking out, disgusted with baseball for being so hard.

"But it's *not* a math test," Kyle would reply. "It's *baseball.* In baseball, batting .400 is *really good*."

But *really good* was for yesterday. A *perfect* batting average was 1.000, which meant getting a hit *every single time* you came up to bat. Ben was no longer interested in anything less.

2. Play "Clair de lune" without making a single mistake.

Ben also loved playing piano and especially the song "Clair de lune," which was so beautiful that it shot shivers through his fingers and toes every time he heard it. Ben wanted to learn how to play "Clair de lune" without messing up once. He had practiced a lot but still made plenty of mistakes.

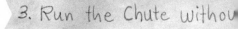

Ben *also* loved riding his scooter. He *wanted* to have the skill and strength and guts to ride down the Chute, which was a famously difficult and diabolically dangerous obstacle course down the hill behind Honeycutt Mall.

To run the Chute, you had to go over two jumps and around a hairpin turn and through a patch of loose gravel before ducking under a low-hanging branch—all while speeding downhill!

Some afternoons, Ben and Janet would take the long way home from school so they could watch an extremely large and frequently irritable fifth grader named Flegg McEggers attempt to run the Chute.

Flegg was strong and fearless. He practiced every day. And even Flegg usually messed up a jump or wiped out in the gravel or rammed his bike into Dead Man's Tree. Flegg's one goal in life was to master the Chute.

Ben wanted to do it, too. *Perfectly.*

Ben didn't love math, but he definitely thought it was interesting. He loved the *ideas* behind math but always got caught up in the *numbers themselves,* so he often messed up a problem even when he understood exactly how it worked.

Which meant he sometimes even missed one of the *non-impossible* questions in addition to the impossible one.

But now that he knew it *was* possible to get a perfect score, Ben wanted to do it himself. He thought Mr. P. was the coolest and wanted Mr. P. to think *he* was the coolest, too.

Ben looked at his list and realized it wasn't *quite* finished.

5. Convince Janet to get to the corner on time.
6. Make Mom a better cook.
7. Fix Dad's lip balm problem.

Ben leaned back in his chair with a smile. The list was *perfect*! Suddenly anything seemed possible.

All he had to do was anything and everything Darbino suggested. And then, once he was perfect himself, Ben would fix everyone else.

CHAPTER 6

After school, Ben went out front to where he always met Janet for their walk home.

"Ready?" she asked with a smile.

Ben loved Janet. She was his best friend in the world. But as he looked at her standing there, he saw how completely imperfect she was.

It wasn't just that she was late all the time. Her glasses were crooked and her hair was a mess. In addition to being covered with crusty dried yogurt, her sweater had several large holes. Her elbow was scraped, her socks didn't match, and one of her shirtsleeves was longer than the other.

Janet needed help.

It was up to Ben to get things started.

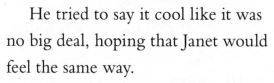 **Sorry,** he said.

I'm going to Darby's today.

He tried to say it cool like it was no big deal, hoping that Janet would feel the same way.

Instead, she seemed surprised and a little bit mad.

I didn't know you guys were friends.

It's a budding relationship.

Why didn't you tell me earlier?

I forgot, said Ben, wondering if he looked sweaty and cross-eyed.

I don't buy it, said Janet.

What's going on?

Janet hated lies more than she hated mosquitoes, and she hated mosquitoes a lot. Ben reminded himself that today's tiny fib was going to help her just as much as it was going to help him.

"The reason I'm going over to Darby's is that . . . we're working on a great big surprise for *you*."

Janet squinted at Ben like a baker squints at a lopsided cake.

He briefly considered sharing his plan to make her perfect but worried she might have trouble realizing how great a plan it was. Janet could be a little too sure of herself. And a lot stubborn.

"See you tomorrow, though," said Ben.

Okay, said Janet with a look that was like a club sandwich stacked high with alternating layers of disappointment and suspicion. She shuffled away down the sidewalk.

Ben waited, and eventually Darby appeared.

"Sorry," he said. "I was reviewing the rules of pronoun usage with Mr. Piscarelli."

"Okay," said Ben. "Why?"

"Because I think they're interesting. And because I want to learn to use them perfectly."

There it was again! Ben's favorite word. He reached into his pocket and gave his fortune a squeeze.

Ready?

Ben asked, as excited as Dumbles when someone dropped an unburnt pancake on the floor.

Ready! Darby was also excited. Ben was glad to see it.

Where do you live?

Emerson and Lake.

Oh, said Ben.

That was the fancy part of town.

They had walked halfway down the block before Ben realized they could save themselves a lot of time by cutting across the street.

Let's cross here, Ben suggested.

Let's *continue to the corner* and use the crosswalk, Darby insisted.

Being perfect means following the rules.

Even the dumb ones? asked Ben, half joking and half not.

There were lots of dumb rules that seemed designed to make kids' lives harder.

"Every rule exists for a reason," said Darby, "even the ones that seem dumb." Ben remembered Darby's request to do exactly what he asked—even if it didn't seem to make sense. If being perfect meant walking a little farther down the street, Ben was willing to do it.

"But . . . ," Darby continued. "If you're perfect *enough,* you can sometimes *change* the rules."

"What do you mean?" Ben liked how that sounded. "What rules have you changed?"

"Well, I used to have a bedtime, but now I'm allowed to stay up as late as I want."

Ben's mind went wild! His parents made him go to bed at 8:00 p.m.!

How did you pull that off?

"By convincing them I was responsible enough to go to bed when I got tired and that I would always be sufficiently alert and agreeable in the morning."

"Wow." Ben wondered if he had *ever* been sufficiently alert and agreeable in the morning. "What else?"

"I'm allowed to spend as much money as I want to on books."

"As much as you want?"

Darby nodded.

Ben's parents made him take books out of the library. "You must have *hundreds* of books."

"Thousands."

"How did you pull *that* off?"

"I demonstrated my commitment to literacy by composing a critical essay about every book I read and presenting it from memory as an after-dinner family activity."

"Was it you or Darbino who convinced them?" Maybe mind control was another of Darbino's powers!

"I'm not sure," Darby admitted. "I sometimes have trouble keeping things straight."

Ben could only imagine.

They turned the corner from Lesser onto Lake. Suddenly the houses were bigger. The lawns were wider. The shrubs were more carefully trimmed. Ben wanted to live in a neighborhood that looked like this.

"There it is," said Darby, pointing.

Ben looked, then looked again, like a thirsty horse catching sight of a cool, clear river.

Darby's house was absolutely *perfect*.

CHAPTER 7

Darby's lawn was perfectly mowed, with no brown patches or poking-up weeds. The house looked like it belonged in a fairy tale.

Instead of being boring and straight, the driveway curved in the shape of a horseshoe. In one of the gardens was a fountain with water that flowed enthusiastically from the mouth of a lion.

Wow, said Ben.

Wow, wow, wow.

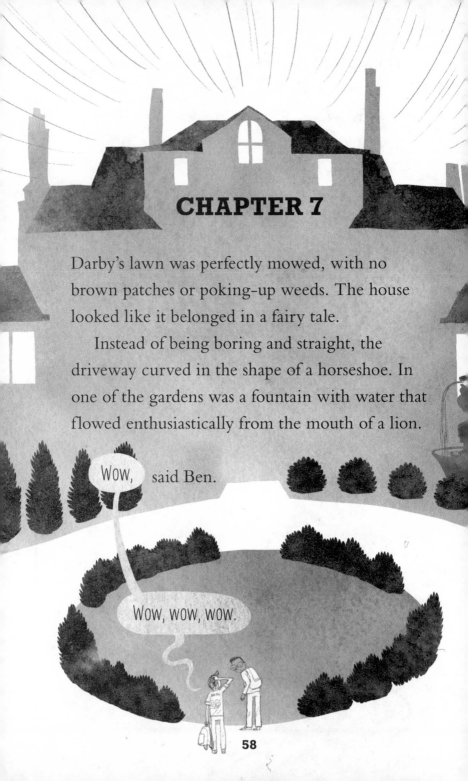

When they got inside, Darby's mom was
waiting with a tray of snacks.

Hello, Darby. Who is this?

She was confident and sure,
like the face on a coin or a stamp.

I'm Ben,

said Ben, holding out his hand as
politely as he could. He wanted
this person to like him.

I'm Simone,

she said, giving his hand a
friendly shake and then
placing the snacks on the table.

Are you boys hungry?

"Yes, please," said Ben, lunging for the snacks as politely as one can possibly lunge. He tried to eat the crackers, cheese, olives, and pepperoni slices with gentlemanly restraint, but it was impossible. Everything was so delicious. Soon all of it was gone.

My goodness, Ben,

said Darby's mom with a chuckle.

You have quite an appetite. Do your parents not feed you?

Ben knew she meant it as a joke, but he suddenly remembered that the pancake disaster had been followed up by an almost inedible tuna fish sandwich in his lunch box.

"We had a *really* small breakfast this morning."

Darby's mom gave Ben a look like an X-ray gives your bones. "Would you like some *cake*?"

Ben felt grateful. Ben felt understood. Ben felt lucky to be alive.

Yes, please.

He ate a piece of carrot cake with cream cheese frosting and almost died from too much happiness.

He tried his hardest *not* to look like he wanted a second slice but must have failed, because Darby's mom served him another, which he gratefully ate before almost dying even *more* happily.

Ben was trying not to look like he wanted a *third* piece when Darby said, "How about we go get started with your lessons?"

Which did the trick. The only thing Ben wanted more than a third piece of cake was to be perfect.

"You boys have fun. I have to get some work done."

Instead of going into the garage and getting into a car and driving away, Darby's mom walked into a room down the hallway.

"I thought she was going to work," said Ben.

"She is," said Darby. "That's her home office. She's a consultant."

"What's that?"

"Someone who helps companies solve problems. People ask Mom questions. She tells them her ideas. She does it from home."

Ben shook his head with dismay. Why didn't *his* parents work from home? He lamented all the afternoon-snack trays he'd missed.

"Come with me," said Darby, who seemed ready to get down to business.

Ben followed him out the back door, across the yard to the base of a tree, up a clever ladder, and into a tree house that had a bunk bed, a dresser, and two hammock chairs.

It was absolutely *perfect*.

WOW,

said Ben, wondering
if he had ever said
"wow" so many
times in one day.

Darby opened a cabinet that contained a mini fridge, inside of which were two cans of Ka-Zing. It was Ben's favorite kind of soda, but he never got to drink it because his parents said it made him act crazy and loud.

Wow, said Ben.

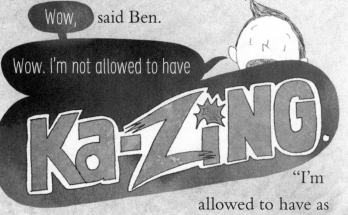

Wow. I'm not allowed to have Ka-Zing.

"I'm allowed to have as much as I want," said Darby in a way that somehow didn't seem like a brag. "All I had to do was convince them that I could drink Ka-Zing without acting all crazy and loud."

Ben didn't understand. "How did you do that?"

"By drinking Ka-Zing and not acting all crazy and loud."

Ben understood the words, but they didn't make sense. What Darby was saying seemed actually impossible. This was *definitely* the work of Darbino.

Darby sat down in one of the hammock chairs and gestured for Ben to sit in the other. They sipped their Ka-Zings and swung back and forth while birds chirped pleasantly in the nearby branches. It should have been the perfect moment.

But Ben wanted more.

"You have that look about you," said Darby, peering intently at Ben like a doctor peers at your tonsils. "I've seen it before. You're ready to start marching down the road to perfection."

"I am! How do we begin?"

"Before we go any further"—Darby leaned forward and gave Ben a long look—"are you absolutely *certain* you want to be perfect?"

Yes! Of course!

Hearing the words made Ben even more excited.

"All right, then. Here we go."

Darby took off his glasses and straightened his back. Even though Ben knew by now what was coming, he still wasn't prepared for the transformation.

"Darbino?"

"Yes, Ben, it's me. You don't need to be nervous."

But Ben couldn't help it.

Darbino stood up and started pacing back and forth, as if hatching an intricate plan.

Perfection is a big objective. Let's start small. What are your goals, Ben?

Ben was glad he'd spent all day thinking about this very question. He pulled out the first page of his list and handed it over.

"All right," said Darbino. "First up, baseball. You want to bat 1.000. That seems perfectly doable."

Ben's heart was a bottle rocket. "It *does*?"

"I don't see why not. Let's head down to the yard."

As they climbed back down the ladder, Ben wondered how in the world Darbino was going to make him a better batter.

Would he teach Ben to read the pitcher's mind?

Would he give Ben superhuman arm strength?

Or extraordinary speed?

"Let's practice," said Darbino. "As your fortune suggests, it's one route to perfection. Lots and lots of practice."

Ben liked practicing baseball, but he wasn't as excited about practicing calculus. Especially not *lots and lots*. "Does that mean there's *another* route to perfection?"

"There is," said Darbino. "But only as a last resort. Let's try practice first."

"Okay." Ben was curious but decided to be patient.

Ben followed as Darbino walked to the garage, took a Wiffle ball and bat off a shelf, and returned to the yard with the look of a coach who expects your best effort.

Darbino threw the ball. He was an extremely good pitcher. Which made sense! He threw ten pitches, and Ben hit two of them. Which was exactly his average.

Then Darbino threw ten more pitches, and Ben hit one.

Ben was discouraged.

"Keep trying," said Darbino. "Perfection doesn't happen all at once." He threw ten more pitches. This time, Ben hit three.

"See?" said Darbino. He threw the ball again and again. Ben hit it sometimes, but mostly he missed. After an hour, he was still hitting the ball only 20 percent of the time.

They sat down to rest. It was a surprisingly warm afternoon.

This isn't working. Do you have any insider tips or secret techniques?

I'm afraid I don't know much about baseball.

But you said—

To be clear, I *could* bat 1.000 if I wanted to. I just don't really want to. Do *you* want to, Ben?

"Of *course!*"

"Are you *sure?*"

The question was so strange that Ben didn't know what to say. The answer *seemed* obvious, but . . . maybe it *wasn't?*

"Here's the thing, Ben. I love calculus. I *love* it. I love it so much that I spend every afternoon reading about it and practicing it. I even *dream* about it."

Ben couldn't imagine dreaming about math.

"Achieving perfection takes your whole heart. Maybe you can't play baseball perfectly because you just don't love it *enough.*"

Ben played tug-of-war with himself. Of *course* he loved baseball! But . . . maybe he just *thought* he did. Maybe he *didn't* love it enough?

Darbino gave Ben a serious look. "Batman doesn't waste his time knitting scarves, does he? Wonder Woman doesn't sit on her porch playing banjo."

Ben had to admit Darbino had a point.

"No! Superheroes save their energy for the things they care about most. Which allows them to focus on doing those things *perfectly*!"

Ben tried to take it all in. The idea was so big that it didn't quite fit inside his head.

"Is this the *other* road to perfection? Giving things up? Because that seems kind of sad."

"I'm afraid so," said Darbino. "But it's only sad at first. Once you realize you're just giving up things you don't actually love, it's kind of a relief."

Ben tried to feel relieved about giving up baseball. But it wasn't working.

"I think that's enough for your first lesson," said Darbino, putting his glasses back on.

Once he was back to his slouching, rumpled self, Darby took the Wiffle ball and bat and put them back in the garage. "I guess we don't need those anymore," he said. "Meanwhile, it's time for breakfast."

Ben's brain replied,

But isn't it dinnertime?

And his stomach asked,

Will there be pancakes?

And his heart wondered,

Is it possible that I actually don't love baseball?

CHAPTER 8

A few minutes later, Ben was staring at a plate of perfect pancakes. Right next to it was a bowl of perfect sausages. Not eight sausages or ten sausages, but a towering mountain.

"What's happening?" asked Ben, who actually couldn't tell if he was dreaming.

"Breakfast for dinner!" Darby replied. "We do it every Monday night."

Ben loved the idea. As far as food themes went, it was so much better than *Monday Meals with Mom!*

May I offer you some sausages, Ben?

asked Darby's dad. He was tall and handsome, with a voice like a tuba. He had a mustache so impressive it might have won a wrestling match.

"Yes," said Ben, his whole heart lunging with joy.

"How many would you like?"

Ben didn't even know what to do with the question. At home, there was a strict limit of three. Sausages came eight to a pack, so Ben got three, his dad got three, and his mom got two, and that was how it always was.

Ben always *wanted* more than three.
Ben always wanted . . .

Eleven?

Darby's dad chuckled. "How about we start with four, and you help yourself if you want more?"

"Sure," said Ben.

"This is one hungry guy," said Darby's mom, who was pouring everyone glasses of something with bubbles.

"What's that?" Ben asked.

"Club soda," said Darby. "It helps with digestion."

"Would anyone like a twist of lime?" asked Darby's dad.

"Yes, please," said Darby. "It's quite refreshing," he explained to Ben.

"Yes, please," said Ben, who figured good digestion and refreshing beverages must be essential parts of living the perfect life.

Darby dropped a slice of lime into Ben's glass.

Darby's parents sat down and reached out with open palms as if they were asking for pocket change. It took Ben a second to realize that *everyone was going to hold hands,* which *seemed extremely weird* but was *maybe the way things worked in a perfect world.*

Ben held hands with Darby's mom and Darby's dad and didn't know what to expect.

We are grateful for this food and for our health and for Darby's friend Ben joining us tonight.

Darby's mom gave Ben's hand a squeeze and then let go.

Shall we eat?

Ben just barely stopped himself from cheering out loud as he picked up his fork and knife and cut into the pancakes. Not only were they exactly circular and just the right amount of golden brown, but they were fluffy and light and cooked to perfection.

Ben took a bite. The taste was just right. The texture was ideal. There was a hint of something magical. "What is that amazing flavor?" *Ben had to know!*

"Almond," said Darby's mom, who was ready for the question. "It's my grandma's recipe."

Ben's eyes made actual tears. The pancakes were just that good.

Are you okay?

asked Darby's mom.
Her voice was
gentle and kind.

I'm all right,

said Ben.

It's just that these pancakes are . . .

"Perfect?" said Darby, giving Ben a sly wink.

"*More* than perfect," said Ben, wondering if it was even possible.

Darby's mom laughed. "Ben, you are welcome here *any*time."

Anytime!

Ben's heart sang in eight-part harmony.

"How was your day, Darby?" she asked.

"I got a perfect score on my math test."

"Of course you did," said Darby's dad. He said it like Darby was talking about something as simple as raking leaves.

"You don't understand," said Ben. "No one has *ever* gotten a perfect score on one of Mr. P.'s math tests. There's always one impossible question."

"No problem is impossible if you know how to solve it," Darby's dad replied.

"What *else* did you two do today?" asked Darby's mom. "That *isn't* about tests or grades?"

"How did *you* do on the test, Ben?" asked Darby's dad before anyone else could reply.

Charles!

Darby's mom gave Darby's dad a look.

But he didn't seem to notice.

Instead, he continued to look at Ben, waiting for him to answer.

"I did okay," said Ben. "Eight out of ten. Which means I only missed one of the non-impossible questions."

"Good job, Ben," said Darby's mom.

"Why do you think you missed it?" asked Darby's dad, not in a way that was disapproving or unkind, but like he actually didn't understand that missing questions on a math test was something that could happen, and he wanted to know how it worked.

"I guess I'm not . . . perfect?" Ben suggested, shrugging his shoulders. Because it was a short-term problem, he didn't mind admitting it.

"Don't worry. No one is," said Darby's mom, patting Ben's hand reassuringly.

"*Almost* no one," said Darby's dad, giving Darby a wink.

Darby's mom frowned. "Would you like some more sausages, Ben?"

Ben had three more sausages. They were absolutely *perfect*.

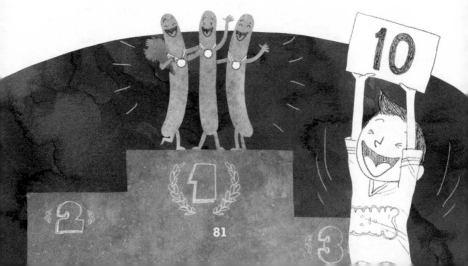

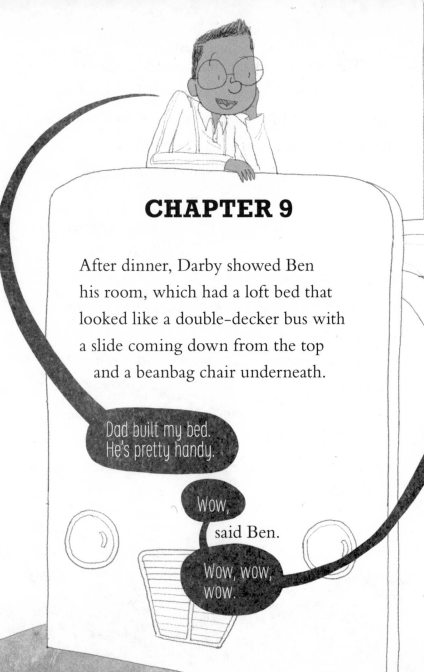

CHAPTER 9

After dinner, Darby showed Ben
his room, which had a loft bed that
looked like a double-decker bus with
a slide coming down from the top
and a beanbag chair underneath.

Dad built my bed.
He's pretty handy.

Wow,

said Ben.

Wow, wow,
wow.

Ben's dad had once installed a shelf in their living room, but it was crooked and sometimes fell off the wall.

It's not *just* Darbino, you know. Do you realize that *everything* in your life is . . . ?

I do realize,

said Darby.

And I try not to take it for granted.

"I assume your parents know—"

"About Darbino? *No.*" Darby's face grew serious and grim. "And they *can't.* Dad wouldn't like it if he knew a superhero was taking my math tests for me."

"But . . ." Ben tried to do the math. "Isn't Darbino also . . . *you?*"

Darby looked pained, as if Ben had just asked him to explain the meaning of the word "nonplussed" or to describe the flavor of nutmeg.

It's . . . extremely . . . complicated.

Ben could tell Darby wanted to change the subject, so he turned to another question that had been tumbling around in his head.

"Where did you go to school before?" This wasn't the bedroom of someone who had just moved to town.

"HONEYCUTT ACADEMY,"

said Darby abruptly, like someone shutting a window because it's starting to rain.

The academy was a private school. Ben's parents had thought about sending him there so he could study Japanese. But it was way too expensive. "Why did you switch?"

Darby answered slowly, choosing his words as if each one cost a dollar.

The kids weren't very nice to me. My parents thought I could use a fresh start.

Ben could tell there was more to the story but sensed that Darby wasn't interested in telling it.

What's that?

Ben asked, pointing to a
fish tank without any water.

"My chameleon, Zanzibar,"
said Darby, clearly relieved that
Ben had changed the subject.
"He's probably hiding. He's
definitely the perfect pet."

Oh yeah?

Ben peered into the tank and spotted a tail
poking out from under a rock. He agreed that
lizards were cool but had always figured that
Dumbles was the perfect pet.

"Absolutely," said Darby.
"They're easy to care for
and have a long life span.
As opposed to hamsters,
which live an average of
2.5 years. That's a lot of
unnecessary sadness."

STILL
KICKIN'!

IT WAS
A GOOD
RUN!

"But what about cuddles and licks?" Dumbles was a champion of cuddling and licking.

"Licks are not sanitary," said Darby. "And cuddles are not necessary."

Ben liked licks. And even if they weren't technically *necessary,* cuddles were extremely *enjoyable.*

"Shall we get back to your lessons?"

Ben looked up, and there, with no warning, was Darbino, holding Ben's list.

"Whoa!" said Ben, shocked and excited all over again.

"Sorry. You'll get used to it eventually."

Ben wasn't sure.

"Okay," Darbino continued, "you want to play 'Clair de lune' perfectly. Admirable goal. My first suggestion would be to practice, but you said you're already doing that. Which makes me wonder, Are you sure you *love* playing piano?"

"Yes!" said Ben with such certainty that Darbino raised both of his eyebrows at once. There was no way Ben was giving up piano.

"Okay! I believe you. So, if practice isn't working, do you know anyone who might be able to help you with your *technique*?"

Ben didn't even have to think about that.

I do.

"Great," said Darbino, turning back to the list. "Start there and report back to me. What's the Chute?"

"A terrifying and possibly deadly obstacle course behind the mall."

"Why do you want to run the Chute, Ben?" Darbino looked at Ben like an astronomer gazes at a distant star.

Ben thought about that. He wasn't sure. "Because . . . *it's there*?"

Darbino nodded. "I've heard worse reasons for wanting to do something. But . . ." He paused, and Ben leaned in. It was a dramatic and exciting moment that seemed extremely important. "It sounds like you don't believe it's possible."

Honestly, I'm afraid
I'd break both my legs,

Ben admitted.

"This could be a problem," said Darbino.
"There's no way that *Darby* could ever do the
backflip I showed you in the schoolyard today.
Because he doesn't *think* he can. But *I*
believe I can do it with every speck of
my being. Which is why I'm able to.
Do you see what I mean?"

Ben nodded. This made
sense.

"So, let me ask you again. Do you
believe you can run the Chute, Ben?"
"Not really?"
Darbino gave Ben an encouraging nod.
"Admitting this is an important first step.
Your assignment is to work on *believing* you
can do it. Picture yourself on your scooter
going down the Chute. See yourself getting
to the bottom *without* two broken legs.
As soon as you believe you *can* do it,
you'll be *able* to."

Ben was amazed. He had no idea it would be so easy! "Okay!" he said. He couldn't wait to get started.

Darbino was reading Ben's list again. "All right. Last item. You want to get a perfect score on Mr. P.'s math test?"

"Yes," said Ben.

"Do you *love* calculus, Ben?"

"I don't know for sure. I *think* I might."

I think you might, too. Calculus is just . . .

$$\int x^2 dx$$

beautiful.

Darbino's eyes were alive with excitement. "There's only one way to find out."

Darbino went over to a bookshelf and pulled down four fat books. "Here," he said, handing them to Ben. "Read these. Start with this." It was called *Calculus for Chuckleheads.*

The books were heavy in Ben's arms. They felt like a responsibility. When it came to calculus, he was much more interested in the *perfect* part than he was in the *practice.* But he didn't want to admit that to Darbino.

Instead, he said, "Thanks!"

"No problem," said Darbino. "Anytime."

The word "time" jogged Ben's memory. He looked at his watch. His parents would be expecting him back from Janet's soon.

"Can one of your parents—I mean *Darby's* parents—drive me home?"

"Sure," said Darbino, sliding his glasses back on. "I'll go ask."

Darby left the room, and Ben slumped down into the beanbag chair. He thought about the past few dizzying hours. Darby's perfect room. The perfect tree house. Those perfect pancakes.

Ben was glad to see what a perfect house looked like. He was relieved to know it was possible to have perfect parents.

Darby came back.

Dad says he'll drive you.

Great. One more question first. Did you have to train your parents to be so perfect?

Nope. They've always been this way.

It made sense to Ben. In the same way that Mrs. Ezra's perfect apple tree grew perfect apples, Darby was amazing because his parents were.

"What if my parents aren't perfect . . . *yet*?"

"You have to convince them that they *want* to be perfect. And they have to be *willing* to do the hard work."

Ben wasn't worried about that. Who wouldn't want to be perfect? He assumed it just hadn't occurred to his parents to try. They were always telling *him* to work hard. Of course they would be willing to do it themselves.

And if they needed his help, Ben would teach them everything Darbino was teaching him. They would be the perfect family!

"I see what you're thinking," said Darby, placing his hand gently on Ben's shoulder. "But don't get your hopes up."

"Why not?"

"I've tried to help people before, but so far no one has been willing to make the necessary sacrifices. Perfection is a lonely road."

Ben was determined. Ben was willing. "I won't let you down! Before long, I'll be perfect right along with you."

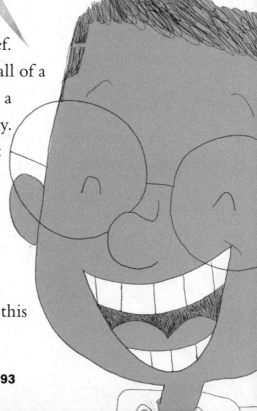

That would be so great!

said Darby with excitement . . . and relief.

He looked different all of a sudden, and it took Ben a second to figure out why. It was the first time that Darby had really smiled since they'd met, and it made him look like a whole new person all over again.

Not just a superhero this time, but a happy one.

CHAPTER 10

Darby's dad drove Ben home, and Darby stayed behind to do his homework.

"Darby tells me you're interested in mathematics," said Darby's dad as he drove his perfect car out of the perfect driveway. He said "mathematics" the way Ben might have said "extremely gooey cinnamon rolls."

"Oh yes. *Extremely*." Ben tried his hardest to believe it.

"I understand completely. Mathematics is the only true science. One might even call it perfect."

Ben's ears perked up. "What do you mean?"

"Mathematics helps us make sense of the world. It gives us clear-cut answers. I find it absolutely beautiful."

"Oh," said Ben, who felt the same way about key lime pie.

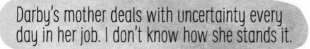

Darby's mother deals with uncertainty every day in her job. I don't know how she stands it.

What do *you* do?

I teach mathematics.

That made sense to Ben.

Because you love it?

Oh yes. I certainly do.

When Darby's perfect dad pulled into Ben's imperfect driveway, Ben was embarrassed about the unmowed lawn and the sagging gutters and the uneven bushes. But Darby's dad didn't mention them.

Because he's perfectly polite, thought Ben as he said, "Thank you," and headed inside.

Who was that?

asked Ben's mom, who was waiting at the door with suspicious eyes and a greasy spatula.

I thought you were at Janet's.

I went over to Darby's after school.

Who?

Darby Washington. He's new.

You are supposed to walk home with *Janet*, mister.

I know. But Darby hasn't made any friends yet. I was trying to make him feel *welcome*.

Ben could see his mom's mad-as-heck face crumbling into her *Well, okay then* face.

"Well, okay then. But next time, ask us first."

"I definitely will," said Ben, surprised that he was getting off the hook so easily and wondering if his mom was slightly less imperfect than she had been that morning.

Ben followed her into the kitchen. Things were happening in various skillets and pots. Things that looked and smelled worrisome.

Ben's mom was smiling like the ringmaster of a precarious circus that was going just well enough.

It's almost time to eat. Your dad should be here any minute.

She was stirring something and flipping something else.

"Great," said Ben, who was almost always up for a second meal.

He sat down at the table with *Calculus for Chuckleheads*. Even though it was technically for beginners, it was almost like trying to read Japanese. Ben wanted to want to learn Japanese . . . just like he wanted to want to learn calculus.

Ben's dad walked in from the garage.

"Just in time," said Ben's mom. *"Monday Meals with Mom!* is happy to present an extravagant feast of tomato soup and grilled cheese!" She lifted a plateful of sandwiches with a frantic smile. "And, just for fun, I didn't burn them!"

Ben's dad clapped. Ben hoped for the best. He took a close look at the plate.

Amazingly, instead of being a sooty disaster, the sandwiches were golden brown! Cheese was oozing temptingly from between the slices of perfectly toasted bread!

The fortune was working its *Magic!*

Ben picked up his sandwich and took an enthusiastic bite. The familiar taste of charcoal filled his mouth. Ben turned his sandwich over. The bottom was as burnt and black as a log in a campfire.

Surprise!

said Ben's mom with a face that was trying its hardest to be a smile.

What I meant to say was that I only burned *one* side!

Usually, the smile would have made everything okay. But now that Ben knew perfect meals were possible, he could no longer eat half-incinerated food.

He put down his sandwich and leaned back in his chair.

What's the matter?

his dad asked.

Aren't you hungry?

Actually, I already ate,

said Ben like it was no big deal.

At Darby's.

Oh?

said Ben's mom with a look that was jealous and wistful and mad.

What did you have?

"Pancakes."

"For *dinner*?"

"Darby's family eats breakfast food for dinner every Monday."

"How fun," said Ben's dad with a genuine smile. "We should try that sometime."

"Maybe we will," said Ben's mom with a genuine frown.

"The pancakes were *so* good," said Ben. "They might even have been . . . *perfect*." Ben lingered on the word "perfect," giving his mom a chance to hear how appealing it sounded.

"Is that so?" she said with a frown that was even more genuine than the first one.

Ben was disappointed. His mom was not taking advantage of her golden opportunity to be inspired.

He sat there while his parents gnawed miserably at their half-burnt sandwiches.

"Do we have any club soda?" he asked, trying to sound casual.

His parents gave him a look.

"No, Ben," said Ben's mom, like he'd asked if they owned a poodle named Xander. "But we do have some *delicious* tap water."

"How about a twist of lime?"

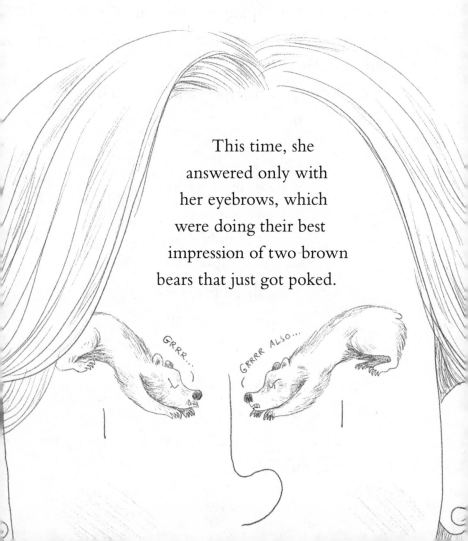

This time, she answered only with her eyebrows, which were doing their best impression of two brown bears that just got poked.

Ben knew there was no lime. He was just being grumpy. And trying to make a point.

They sat there in silence, neither holding hands nor discussing the beauty of mathematics. There was no perfect cake waiting on the counter to make everything okay.

Dumbles scratched at the door, and Ben's mom let him in. Dumbles took a running leap, landed in Ben's lap, and proceeded to shower him with cuddles and licks.

Ben *wanted* to enjoy the cuddles and licks. Instead, he said,

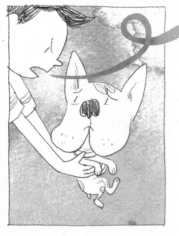

No, Dumbles!

and put Dumbles on the floor.

Dumbles gave Ben a look like a sheep gives the farmer right after its haircut.

"What did he do?" asked Ben's mom, offended on Dumbles's behalf.

"Licks are unsanitary," said Ben. "And cuddles are unnecessary."

Ben's mom leaned over and put her hand on Ben's forehead. "Who *are* you? And what have you done with our Ben?"

"*I* am Ben. And I am dissatisfied."

Ben's mom gave him a look like a spider gives a fly that's thrashing around in her web.

Go on.

Ben had so much to say, but he couldn't find the right words. So he pulled out his fortune and handed it to his mom.

Practice makes perfect.

"Why are you showing this to *me*?" she asked, seeming to know the answer but unwilling to admit it.

"I just thought you might find it . . . helpful," said Ben, like someone who is walking on a frozen lake and hoping the ice is thick enough.

"What are you trying to say, Ben?"

Her mood was a concrete wall, and Ben was a rubber hammer that stood no chance of making a dent.

They stared at each other for a few tense moments, and to Ben's surprise, his mom crumbled first.

Cooking without burning things is really hard!

I believe you,

said Ben.

I just thought the fortune was really inspiring. I hoped you'd be *inspired.*

I'm tired, is what I am.

Maybe making unburnt pancakes would be easier if you . . .

practiced?

Whatever embers had been quietly smoldering in her heart burst suddenly into a full-blown blaze.

"What do you think I've been doing, Ben? I have been practicing *every single Monday* so that I can be a better cook! Do you think it feels great to make food that not even Dumbles will eat?"

Ben thought he knew the answer, but he wasn't *quite* sure.

No?

Ding! Ding! Ding!

NO

That is correct, Ben! It does not feel great. But I am *trying.*

BEN

$1,000

Ben knew it was time to let go, but instead he continued to squeeze. "Maybe you need to try . . . *harder?*"

Ben's mom got the look a spider makes when the thrashing fly breaks free and the web falls completely apart. It was a look Ben hoped he'd never have to see again.

"That is a pretty lousy thing to say to your mother, mister." She stood up so quickly that she knocked over her chair. She stormed out of the room and thumped up the stairs and slammed the bedroom door so hard the house shook.

And then it was finally quiet.

Ben looked at his dad.

His dad looked at him.

"Here's the thing," said his dad.

"What?" Ben knew he'd done something wrong, but he didn't know how to make it right again.

If you want to get better at baseball, you can go to the batting cage and work on your swing, and it doesn't really matter if you hit the ball or not, because you're just practicing. But parents have to practice while the actual game is happening.

Moms have to wake up every morning and try not to burn the pancakes. Dads have to remember to take the lip balm out of their pants in the middle of all the other things they're trying to do and remember each day.

Lip Balm

"It's the same for kids!" said Ben, who still wasn't ready to forgive his parents for his incredibly difficult morning. "We have to get up and eat those burnt pancakes and wear greasy, wet jerseys to school."

"That's true," said Ben's dad. "Which is a great opportunity for you to *practice* being patient and understanding with your imperfect parents."

Ben didn't want to be patient *or* understanding.

"Which reminds me that I've been meaning to thank you," said Ben's dad, who had a sparkle in his eye that Ben knew meant trouble.

"What for?"

"For giving *me* so many opportunities to practice being patient and understanding."

"What do you mean?"

"All those times when you left the toilet seat up and forgot to clear your plate and didn't remember to put the milk back in the fridge and ate the last cookie without throwing away the box and—"

"Okay, okay. I get it," said Ben, who had heard enough about his various shortcomings. "You are a master of patience and understanding."

"I think your mom is doing pretty well, too."

"Yeah," said Ben. He had to admit that no matter how far from perfect his mom might be, she did try really hard.

"You think maybe you could go tell her that?"

Yeah,

said Ben again, not really very interested in saying he was sorry but knowing it was probably the right thing to do.

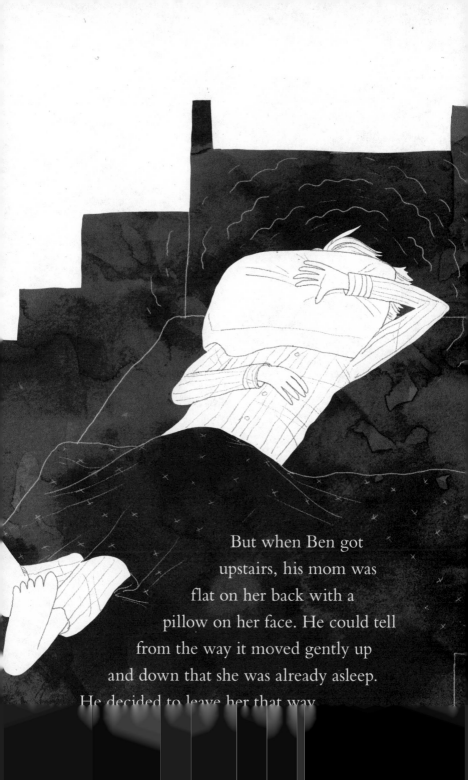

But when Ben got
upstairs, his mom was
flat on her back with a
pillow on her face. He could tell
from the way it moved gently up
and down that she was already asleep.
He decided to leave her that way.

CHAPTER 11

Ben woke up so early the next morning that it was still dark as he got himself dressed, walked two houses down the block, and knocked.

A moment later, the door burst open, and there was the smiling face of their neighbor Mrs. Ezra, maker of cakes, grower of enchanted apples, and quite possibly a witch. Her dog, Felicity, yipped and wriggled happily against Ben's ankles. It took every shred of his willpower to stop himself from bending down to get some cuddles and licks.

Every Tuesday morning, Ben had a piano lesson. When he'd asked Mrs. Ezra to teach him, she'd insisted the lessons be first thing in the morning. Not just before school and not just before breakfast, but before Ben was even fully awake.

"It is the very best time to learn piano," she'd explained.

So there Ben was, with the moon still high above his head, holding his sheet music for "Clair de lune."

Good morning,

said Mrs. Ezra far more cheerfully than seemed possible before sunrise.

What shall we work on today?

Ben got right to the point. "I want to learn how to play 'Clair de lune' *perfectly*."

"Why?" Mrs. Ezra squinted at Ben like a wise old raisin squints at a grape.

Ben took out his fortune and handed it to her.

I see, she said.

And what do you mean by "perfectly"?

Ben was surprised by the question. "Everyone knows what 'perfectly' means."

"Oh good. If *everyone* knows, then you do, too. What does it mean to be perfect, Ben?"

Often, Mrs. Ezra's questions floated toward you like icebergs that were quite a bit larger than they seemed on the surface.

But this didn't seem to be one of those times.

Because *perfect* was not a confusing concept.

When you do something without making any mistakes.

So, you want to play "Clair de lune" without making any mistakes?

Yes.

Then we have a problem.

Why?

Because you can't play something perfectly until you stop wanting to.

That didn't make any sense. Which was pretty much what Ben expected when it came to Mrs. Ezra.

But I *can't* make myself stop wanting to.

Then maybe I can,

said Mrs. Ezra.

Follow me.

She opened a small green door and marched Ben into a room that he'd always wondered about but hadn't ever been invited to visit.

The room was not much larger than a closet. Against the wall was an upright piano. Mrs. Ezra gestured to the bench. "Sit."

Ben sat.

"Play."

Ben played. But nothing happened when he pressed down on the keys.

It's broken.

Mrs. Ezra gave Ben a disapproving scowl. "Would I ask you to play a broken piano? This is an entirely functional and extremely *magical* piano. This piano was made for people who want to learn to play *perfectly*."

Ben gave a wide-eyed gasp. *He had come to the right place!* But . . . "If I can't hear myself play . . . ?"

"Then you'll have to use a *different* set of ears."

As far as Ben knew, he had only one set, but before he could point this out, Mrs. Ezra had moved on.

"You will play and play and play until your fingers know the notes so well that they don't need your ears' permission to do their job properly. This method is called 'blueprinting.' I usually reserve it for my most dedicated adult students, because it is difficult. It only works if you are *hungry*."

"I'm always hungry."

"I'm not talking about cake, Ben. When it comes to piano, so far, you have only been hungry-*ish*."

Ben tried not to be offended.

"This morning, you finally seem hungry *enough*."

"What do I do?"

"Play."

"But how do I—?"

"Play!"

Ben played. Playing without sound was disorienting. "But how will I know if I'm making mistakes?"

"*I* can hear them. Let *me* be your other set of ears for now."

Mrs. Ezra sat next to Ben as he played, watching his fingers and pointing out when he hit the wrong key or messed up the rhythm.

Before long, a funny thing happened. Because Ben couldn't hear, he slowed down. Because he slowed down, he made fewer mistakes.

Maybe Mrs. Ezra was onto something. But . . .

I miss hearing the notes.

"Do you want to learn to play 'Clair de lune' perfectly, Ben?"

"Yes."

"Then play it in silence for now."

"Okay."

"The road to perfection can be lonely."

It was pretty much the same thing Darby had said!

Mrs. Ezra kept going.

That's why so few people decide to walk in that direction. But if you are determined to try, I will walk with you.

They played like that for a long time. As Ben's brain built a bridge between the notes on the page and the work of his fingers, he heard nothing but the gentle thumping of unstrung keys and Mrs. Ezra's contented sighs. Eventually, Ben's fingers got tired. Eventually, the sun came up. Eventually, he went home.

CHAPTER 12

As Ben headed back down the block to his house, he decided to apologize to his mom. It seemed like the right thing to do.

As he walked down the hallway toward the kitchen, he smelled something buttery and sweet and not at all burnt. He followed the scent to a plate that held three not-quite-perfect-but-certainly-acceptable pancakes.

"These pancakes look great," said Ben to his dad, thankful that

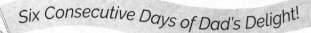

Monday Meals with Mom!

had been replaced by

Six Consecutive Days of Dad's Delight!

Ben wondered if he should make another sign.

"Your *mom* made them," said Ben's dad, pointing across the kitchen to where Ben's mom stood with a spatula and a smile.

"She *did*?"

"I did," said his mom. "And I have *more* great news."

"What's that?" Ben was excited.

Monday Meals with Mom!

has been upgraded to

Mom Cooks Every Single Meal

Until

She Gets It Right!

Ben's plan to apologize got swept away in a torrent of regret. "That's . . . great," he said, trying his hardest to sound like he meant it.

"I thought you'd be excited," said his mom with a look like a person who is trying not to gloat. "You wanted me to *practice,* right?"

Ben wasn't going to admit defeat.

I sure did,

he said, smiling and
nodding and doing his
best impression of
someone who is pleased.

I've been practicing, too,

said Ben's dad, holding
up Ben's jersey, *which
appeared to be free of stains*!

We got a *different* special spray.

Ben took a closer look. The stains were still
there, but they were definitely less noticeable
than they had been before.

"Thanks," he said, trying to focus on the
bright side. Overall, his plan was working. He'd
inspired his parents to practice being perfect, and
they were already making progress.

Which meant it was time to focus on his even
greater challenge.

A few minutes later, Ben was standing on the corner with the yellow bush.

At first, Janet was just late. And then she was *sort of* late. Before long, she was *really* late and then *extremely* late.

Oh man, I'm late, said Janet when she finally showed up.

Instead of being mad, Ben was excited. Janet had provided the perfect opportunity to make his point. But he didn't want to repeat the mistake he'd made with his mom.

He decided to ease into it. "*Since it's so late, I guess we'll have to jog if we want to get to school on time.*" Ben knew Janet hated jogging. It made her miserable and mad.

"I guess so," she said with a smile. "Good thing we're so fast."

It wasn't the reply Ben had been hoping for.

Janet started to sprint.

He had to race to catch up.

For some reason, Janet *wasn't* miserable and mad. She was having fun. She was missing the point entirely.

Hold on a second, said Ben between gasps.

What?

Here,

he said, handing her his fortune and hoping it would help.

Look.

Is this from yesterday's cookie?

Yes,

said Ben, watching Janet's face and waiting for the inspiration to sink in.

But instead, she shrugged her shoulders and handed the fortune back. "Sorry you didn't get a better one."

Ben was horrified. This was not the right response. "It's the wisest fortune I've ever read!"

"Bah," said Janet. "Who wants to be perfect?"

All the candles in Ben's head blew out at once.

All the trees fell over.

All the kittens cried.

"What do you mean?"

"I mean, I *like* things that are messy and broken," Janet explained. "It makes them more *comfortable*. There's nothing worse than walking into a house that's so neat and clean you're afraid to touch anything."

I think it's an *excellent* fortune,

said Ben, desperately trying to help Janet see what she was missing.

In fact, it's making my life much better already.

Janet was clearly intrigued. "How so?"

Ben wasn't ready for this *particular* question. He didn't have any good examples *yet*. But since he knew they were coming, he borrowed one from the future. "Well, for example, my batting average has improved."

"Oh, that's exciting. You've been stuck at .200 for a while. What's your secret?"

"Lots of *practice*."

"But you just got that fortune yesterday!"

"Days are long, Janet."

Janet looked skeptical.

You have a game this afternoon, right?

Yeah.

Great. I'll come watch. I *can't wait* to see your progress.

124

"Oh, you don't have to. I know you're probably busy."

"I'm not busy at all."

Ben decided the time had come to plant the seed. "Don't *you* have some practicing to do?"

Janet's expression was stuck somewhere between mad and confused. "Practicing for *what* exactly?"

"You know, the things you don't do *perfectly*."

Janet looked at Ben like a ravenous jackal who has just decided what to eat for lunch.

What are you referring to *specifically*, Ben?

"I don't know." Ben tried to sound casual. "Like . . . for example . . . *being on time* in the morning."

Janet let out an exasperated sigh. "I have a question for you, Ben. Are we late?"

Ben looked up. They were across the street from the school. He looked down at his watch. Because they had jogged, they were right on time.

"No," he was forced to admit, "but we *are* sweaty."

"Do you know when *else* we get sweaty, Ben? Whenever we play kickball. Which happens e*very single day* at recess. As far as I can tell, me being late today just means you got sweaty a little bit earlier than usual. And for that I am *truly sorry*."

Janet wasn't sorry at all.

I have bad news for you, Ben.

What?

No one is perfect.

But—

And especially not *you*!

Janet stomped off, and Ben stayed put.

His great big plans were falling apart. How was he going to help Janet become perfect if it wasn't even something she wanted?

He needed help. Luckily, he knew *exactly* where to find it.

127

CHAPTER 13

Tuesdays began with social studies.

"I'm going to read you something," said Mr. P. "Extra credit for anyone who can tell me what it is. 'We the people of—'"

Walter's hand shot into the air.

"Yes, Walter?"

The United States Constitution!

"Well done," said Mr. P. with a smile. "Now, who can tell me what the people who wrote the Constitution were trying to *accomplish*?"

Walter raised his hand again, but Mr. P. looked around the room to see if anyone else knew.

Ben was sure Darby
knew, or at least that
Darbino did, but
Darby just sat there,
slumping a little and
pretending to have
no idea.

"Okay," said Mr. P.
"How about I keep reading, and
we'll see if you can figure it out? 'We the people
of the United States, in order to form a more
perfect union, establish justice—'"

Ben raised his hand.

"Yes, Ben?"

Did you just say that
the United States is . . .

perfect?

This was a welcome surprise. It
would be so much easier to be perfect
while living in a perfect country.

Mr. P. laughed. "No, Ben, I'm afraid that this country is not perfect. No country is. When you have a bunch of people trying to get along, there are always going to be challenges. But the Founding Fathers wanted the country to work as well as it could. I think 'more perfect' was their way of saying 'as good as possible.'"

"How did they do it?" asked Ben, hoping the answer, whatever it was, also applied to baseball.

"Well," said Mr. P., "they had a series of meetings and shared lots of ideas and worked together to come up with the best possible system of government."

"Did it work?"

"Yes and no," said Mr. P. "On one hand, our country still has lots of problems. But on the other hand, the Constitution has kept us going for more than two hundred years."

Ben was excited. Perhaps, instead of practicing and giving up things you weren't good at, there was a third road to perfection: having a chat with a bunch of wise citizens.

"Wait," said Janet with her *Listen up because I'm about to make a really good point* voice.

"Yes, Janet?"

"You said '*more* perfect.' That doesn't make any sense. Isn't perfect already as good as it gets?"

"That's a great observation," said Mr. P. " 'Perfect' means 'the best possible version of something.' Another word like it is 'unique,' which means 'the only one of its kind.' You don't need to say '*more* unique.' You're either one of a kind or you're not."

So, what you're saying is the Founding Fathers weren't very good at grammar?

said Janet with a smug smile.

"Here's what I think," said Mr. P., chuckling. "Since they knew that no country could ever be perfect, they used words they hoped would inspire people to be *as perfect as they could.*"

"But basically, you're saying that perfection *isn't* possible?" asked Janet, looking at Ben as she said it.

"When it comes to something as complicated as running a country, I'd say definitely not."

I'm glad you agree, said Janet, folding her arms like a person who just won a ribbon for growing a really big pumpkin.

"But aren't you also saying that we should all *try* to be as perfect as we can?" Ben asked, looking over at Janet as he did.

"When it comes to getting along and treating everyone fairly, I'd say it's *absolutely* worth trying."

I'm glad you agree,

said Ben, folding his arms like a person whose thousand-pound pony just sat on the prizewinning pumpkin.

Ben felt like he had won. He glanced over at Janet, whose face declared that *she* had.

Even though they were having an argument, Ben was proud that Janet was his friend. She was smart. She said what she believed. She wasn't afraid to be disagreed with.

She definitely couldn't have been more unique. But Ben knew in his heart that she could be slightly more perfect.

CHAPTER 14

At recess, instead of playing kickball, Ben sat on the bench with Darby.

It didn't take Janet long to figure out that something funny was going on. Ben watched as she marched over toward the bench, just as he'd hoped she would.

What are you doing? she shouted to Ben.

I'm trying to pick you for my team.

I'm talking with Darby.

Who?

Darby,

said Ben, gesturing
to Darby, who was
sitting right next
to him.

"Oh, hi," said Janet with a
surprised smile, as if Darby had
suddenly appeared out of nowhere.
"Do you want to play, too?"

"No thanks."

"But *you* will, right?" said Janet, looking
at Ben, who had *never* not played kickball.

"Sorry," said Ben. "I'm too busy working
on being perfect."

"Ugh," said Janet. "Weren't you listening to
Mr. P.?"

"I was. And I'm pretty sure he said that
the quest for perfection is important . . . and
inspiring."

"He also said it's impossible!"

"I get why you're skeptical," said Ben. "I was,
too, until . . ."

"Until what?"

135

"Until I met Darby. Like me, you might have assumed that he's just—" Ben stopped himself.

"Just what?" said Janet.

"He was going to say 'boring,'" said Darby.

"I *wasn't*!" Ben protested.

"I *never* assumed that," said Janet.

Before things could get any more awkward, Ben barreled on. "What you don't know is that Darby is actually—"

"What are you doing, Ben?" Darby cut in. "You *promised*."

"Promised *what*?" Janet's impatient voice was suddenly replaced by her curious one.

"Can I talk to you *over there* for a second?" said Darby, nodding toward the little-kid jungle gym.

"Sure," Ben replied. "Don't go anywhere!" he pleaded to Janet.

Janet rolled her eyes. *Twice.*

What's wrong? asked Ben when they were safely out of earshot.

You promised not to tell anyone about Darbino!

"And I never would!"

"You were about to tell Janet!"

"But . . ." Ben was confused. "Janet isn't *any*one! She's *some*one. She's my best friend!"

"When I said no one, I meant absolutely *no one.*"

Ben could tell Darby wasn't going to budge, so he decided to take a different approach. "Janet *needs* you, Darby. She's great, but she could really use some inspiration. I mean, *look* at her."

They looked over at Janet, who was standing there, sweaty and a little bit rumpled.

"I see what you mean," Darby admitted.

"What if I tell her about the perfect parts of you without mentioning Darbino?"

Ben sensed that Darby was starting to waver, so he pressed gently on. "I just want Janet to see how great you are. So you can help her like you're helping me. That's what superheroes *do,* isn't it? I'm pretty sure Darbino would approve."

The thought of making Darbino happy seemed to push Darby over the top.

"Okay. You're probably right. But absolutely no mention of Darbino."

"I swear."

They walked back to where Janet was standing, doing her best impression of an owl that's tired of waiting for sundown.

That was weird. Are you guys okay?

Never better,

said Ben. And then he continued, choosing his words as delicately as someone who's building a house of cards on a breezy afternoon.

Here's the thing: Darby is *really* good at math.

"I assumed that from his perfect score," said Janet. "*Congratulations!* Is that all you wanted to tell me?"

"You don't understand. He's not just *really* good at math. He's actually *really, really* good. He's actually *really, really, really*—"

"Out with it!" said Janet, glancing over her shoulder to see what was happening in the kickball game. "Actually *what?*"

"Perfect," said Darby reluctantly.

"Ugh," said Janet. "You too? What is it with you guys?"

"Don't you see?" Ben pleaded. "Before yesterday, I never knew that perfection was possible. But now that I do—"

"Being good at math doesn't make you perfect," Janet argued.

"Okay, fine, but calculus is just a tiny part of it. There are . . . *other* things, too. *Incredible* things. Things like . . ." Ben battled his urge to shout

DARBINO

at the top of his lungs.

Instead, he said, "You'll just have to trust me."

"Ben, I can tell you're really excited, and that's great, but I have some kickball to play."

Ben knew he would never be able to persuade Janet on his own. He turned to Darby in desperation. "You *have* to show her."

Darby made a face like Ben had asked him to eat an uncooked clam. "Show her . . . what?"

You know, the . . . flip thing.

Janet paused, her curiosity an invisible rope that was keeping her from walking away.

"It won't be enough," Darby protested. "She's not ready to believe."

Janet looked Darby straight in the eye. "Try me."

Without saying a word, Darby took off
his glasses and slid them casually into his shirt
pocket. He stood up straight, flipped up his
collar, and folded his arms in front of his chest.
He was tall, strong, mighty, and confident, an
even more amazing Darbino than Ben had seen
the day before.

"Wow," said Ben, glancing over at Janet. Her
jaw was set like a person determined to walk into
a hurricane. If she felt like saying "Wow," she
wasn't about to admit it.

"You stopped slouching," said Janet. "Is that it?"

Ben winced. This wasn't how it was supposed to go!

"No," said Darbino, rising up to meet the might of Janet's glare. "We're just getting started."

He kicked off his shoes and glanced around to make sure no one else was looking. But everyone else was focused on the game.

Without warning, Darbino sprang into motion. He sprinted across the schoolyard, leaped into the air, and did a thrilling sequence of tumbling, twisting flips before landing with perfect grace and dipping his head in a modest bow.

Whoa! said Janet as Darbino walked back to where they were standing.

That was ... *amazing!*

Thank you, said Darbino.

"You did that . . . *very well*," said Janet. "I don't know enough about gymnastics to say that it was *perfect,* but—"

"It *was*," said Darbino. "If qualified judges had been present, I would have earned a perfect score."

Janet held her tongue but rolled her eyes again. "Well, great job. Have fun, you two. I'm off to play kickball."

"But . . ." Ben didn't know what else he could possibly do to make Janet see. "Don't you want to learn how to be perfect, too?"

Janet shrugged. "I'm not really into gymnastics, and I'm pretty sure I can wait on the fancy-pants math." She started to walk away.

"Wait!" Ben practically shouted. "You might be interested to know that Darby is also perfect at *other* things. Such as . . . *archery*." Ben knew Janet loved archery but that she wasn't very good at it.

"Really?" said Janet, turning to Darbino, who shot Ben a death glare.

"I've never *tried* archery," Darbino admitted.

"But . . . ," said Ben, knowing he was walking on a tightrope, "you *could* do it perfectly if you wanted to, *right*?" Before Darbino could answer, Ben turned to Janet and said, "Darby can do *anything* perfectly if he wants to."

Janet looked at Darbino like a frog looks at a fly. "Let me get this straight. You've never tried archery, but if you did, you would hit the bull's-eye?"

"If I felt like it. I'm just not interested."

"Hmm . . . ," said Janet with a sneer. "That sure is *convenient*."

Darbino glared at Janet. Janet glared at Darbino. It was like watching the pitcher and batter stare each other down when the game is tied and the bases are loaded.

Ben knew he had to break the standoff before someone got injured. "Here's the thing, Janet. Darby has to keep his perfection on the down low. There's a reason Batman wears his Batsuit only when he absolutely has to."

Hold it,

said Janet.

Are you comparing Darby to Batman?

"I can't think of a better analogy," said Ben with a casual shrug. They had been studying analogies. He was excited to have an opportunity to use the word and hoped he had done it correctly.

Janet seemed to be puzzling through it as well. "So . . . are you trying to say that . . . Batman is perfect?"

Ben and Darbino looked at her as if she were speaking Norwegian.

"I don't even know how to respond to that," said Darbino.

"He has an enormous underground cave full of incredible vehicles!" said Ben.

"He can climb skyscrapers!"

"And defeat the most hideous supervillains without breaking a sweat!"

"How much more perfect can you get?"

Ben knew Janet had a Batman poster on her bedroom wall. She was a huge fan. But he could tell she still wasn't convinced.

"Doesn't Batman have some sort of tragic backstory?" Janet argued. "*That* doesn't seem perfect."

"He did have a difficult childhood," Darbino admitted, "but he uses his pain as motivation to do good."

"Right," said Ben. "Without all the hardship, he would probably just sit by his bat-shaped pool eating tiny ears of corn on toothpicks."

Ben loved tiny corn on toothpicks. He only got to have it on extremely fancy occasions.

"Let me make sure I understand what you're saying. . . ." Janet paused. "If someone who definitely *isn't* perfect decides to wear shiny black pants and fight crime, it somehow makes him perfect?"

Janet was a pin looking for a balloon to pop.

Darbino and Ben were grasping for answers when she delivered the death blow.

"Here's what I think. If not even Batman is perfect, then there's no way in heck Darby is!"

Instead of coming up with the perfect reply, Darbino put his glasses back on and slumped even more than usual.

I don't expect you to understand. It's lonely being me.

Janet calmed down a little.

Then why don't you put your shoes back on and come play kickball with the rest of us?

It wouldn't be fair. I'm even better at kickball than I am at calculus.

I bet you're just as perfect at kickball as you are at archery,

said Janet, rolling her eyes and groaning in exasperation.

GROA

She gave Ben a sharp look. "You have a decision to make, Ben Yokoyama. You can either stand here chatting with Batman or you can come have fun with us disappointingly regular people."

"Go ahead if you want to," said Darby. "Or . . . we can continue your lessons."

Ben was torn!

He wanted to go with Janet, but maybe kickball was another thing he'd have to give up in his quest for perfection.

While he was busy not
deciding, Janet walked away.

Come on! Let's
just go play,

Ben pleaded to Darby.

Once they see how
good you are, everyone
will be amazed.

Even Janet.

Darby looked down at his hands. "No, Ben,
like Batman, Darbino only uses his powers for
good. I don't know what my mission is yet, but
I'm pretty sure it isn't beating Kyle at kickball, as
much as I'd enjoy that."

"I understand," said Ben, trying his hardest to
mean it.

Darby raised his head and smiled at Ben. "Just think . . . once we take my powers and add your perfection at baseball, piano, and daredevil scooter riding, we'll be an unstoppable duo!"

"I can't wait," said Ben with the best smile he could manage.

But it was hard to feel good as he watched Janet walk back to the kickball game without him.

"I feel bad for her," said Darby. "The only thing harder than being perfect is being imperfect."

"Yeah," said Ben. But at that moment, he mostly felt bad for himself.

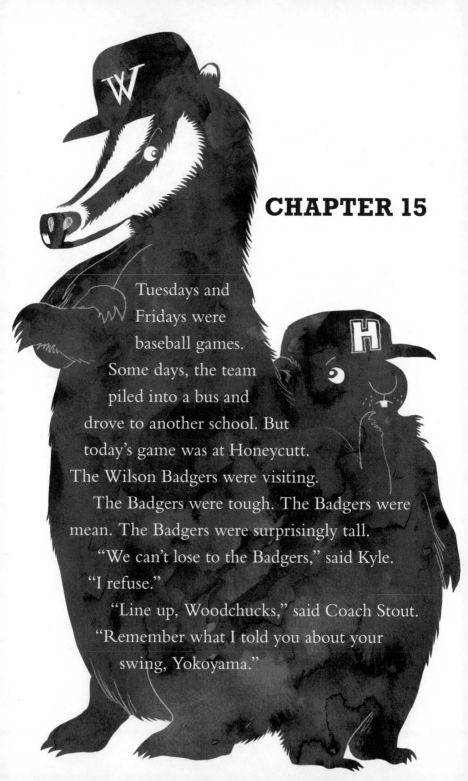

CHAPTER 15

Tuesdays and
Fridays were
baseball games.
Some days, the team
piled into a bus and
drove to another school. But
today's game was at Honeycutt.
The Wilson Badgers were visiting.

The Badgers were tough. The Badgers were
mean. The Badgers were surprisingly tall.

"We can't lose to the Badgers," said Kyle.
"I refuse."

"Line up, Woodchucks," said Coach Stout.
"Remember what I told you about your
swing, Yokoyama."

Coach Stout had told Ben not to think so hard about his swing.

I remember,

said Ben.

Don't think! Just *feel* it!

That's right,

said Coach Stout.

Just *feel* it.

Ben had tried to just *feel* it, but it hadn't worked. Mostly because he had no idea what that actually meant.

The game started well. Kyle hit a single and then scored when Mario hit a double.

Then the Badgers came up to bat and scored two runs on a single and a home run by a kid the size of a yeti.

As the innings marched on, the score swung back and forth. Ben batted twice and struck out twice. He came up to bat in the bottom of the sixth with two outs and a runner on third.

His team was down by a run. Honeycutt Little League games were only six innings long with no extra innings, so this was his final chance. If Ben got a hit, the runner would probably score, meaning his team could do no worse than tie, which was so much better than losing.

Go, Ben, go! shouted Janet from the bleachers.

You can do it, Ben, said Walter, who was even worse at batting than Ben and only got to play when someone was sick.

Just *feel* it, Yokoyama, said Coach Stout.

Ben tried to *feel* it. But instead, he *thought* about how far from perfect Walter was. As soon as he was done helping his parents and Janet, he would help Walter get more perfect, too. It would be his greatest triumph.

The pitcher threw the ball.

STRIKE ONE!

Ben tried to *feel* it. Instead, he *thought* about a particular part of "Clair de lune" where his fingers had to move in such complicated ways that it seemed actually impossible he'd ever get it right.

STRIKE
TWO!

Ben tried to *feel* it. Instead, all he could do was *think* about whether or not his dinner would be edible.

STRIKE
THREE!

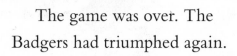

The game was over. The Badgers had triumphed again.

Mario glared at Ben.

Kyle groaned and threw his cap.

Even Walter looked slightly irritated.

Finally, Ben *felt* something. And what he felt was bad.

I don't want to feel bad, he thought. *Feeling bad is so far from perfect.*

As he took off his cleats, Ben reviewed the facts. Darby loved calculus and had practiced until he was perfect.

Ben loved baseball and practiced and practiced but never got any better, which had to mean that . . . Ben saw no other explanation: he didn't love baseball *enough*.

Ben knew what he had to do. He walked over to Couch Stout.

I'm sorry, Coach, but I can't play anymore.

The game is over, Yokoyama. *No one* can play anymore.

"No, I mean . . . *ever*," said Ben, feeling sweaty and cross-eyed, even though he was telling the truth. "I'm quitting the team."

What are you talking about, Ben?

It was Janet, shouting from the other side of the fence. Ben wanted her to butt out.

"There's no shame in losing to the Badgers, Yokoyama." Coach Stout was surprisingly calm.

"It's not that. I just don't . . . *love* baseball anymore."

"These are big words," said Coach Stout. "Are you sure you've thought this through?"

Ben wasn't sure at all. "I am."

"All right, then. Hand over your cap."

Ben wasn't ready for that. Even if he didn't love baseball anymore, he did love his cap. "Do I *have* to?"

"Caps are for Woodchucks. Are you a Woodchuck?"

"Not anymore."

Coach Stout held out his hand. Ben surrendered his cap.

Darby had said there would be sacrifices.

Janet met Ben by the schoolyard gate. "What the double heck, Ben?"

Ben didn't want to talk about it, but he knew Janet wasn't going to let it slide.

"I don't love baseball anymore, okay?"

"Since when?"

"Since a while now."

"Is this because of Darby?"

"Yes . . . and no," said Ben. "He didn't tell me to quit baseball, but he did help me see I don't love it as much as I thought."

"You've always loved baseball," said Janet, "and I'm pretty sure you still do."

Ben stared at the ground.

"If I really loved baseball, I wouldn't have struck out three times," he said, trying to make sense of the last few minutes. "I have to focus on the things I love best."

"Like what?"

Ben wondered what he loved.

When it came to baseball, even though he was supposed to *feel* it, all he could ever seem to do was *think*.

Thinking was for . . .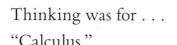

"Calculus."

Janet bristled like someone
who'd just kissed a cactus.

"You love . . . *calculus*? You've
never even mentioned it before."

"I didn't love it before. But I do now."

"*Do* you, Ben?"

"Absolutely."

"All right, then," said Janet. And that was all
she said.

They walked home, side by side but
not really together and not saying a word.
When they got to the corner with the
yellow bush, Janet turned left toward her
house, and Ben watched her walk away, wanting
to say something but not knowing what it was.

He clutched his fortune
and reminded himself:
The road to perfection is lonely.

CHAPTER 16

When he got home, Ben sat down at the kitchen table and pulled out the four fat calculus books. Mr. P.'s math tests were on Wednesdays, which meant he had one night to learn everything.

As he read *Calculus for Chuckleheads,* Ben thought about baseball. Which was strange, since he no longer loved baseball.

It was even stranger how difficult it was for someone who loved calculus as much as Ben did to enjoy reading a book about calculus.

He was having such a hard time loving calculus and not thinking about baseball that he decided to go do the one thing he knew he loved without a single doubt.

Ben walked down the block and knocked on Mrs. Ezra's door. "I wonder if I could play your magical piano for a while."

"Of course," said Mrs. Ezra. "Come in. We have work to do."

"But first, could *you* play it?"

Ben knew his brain and his fingers needed practice,

but his heart needed to hear the actual notes.

"I'd be glad to," said Mrs. Ezra with a smile.

As she sat at the grand piano and began to play, Ben forgot all about baseball and calculus.

Clair de lune meant "light of the moon." And that's how the song made him feel as it poured out of Mrs. Ezra's fingers.

Like he was standing in a field lit by moonlight, looking out at distant mountains on a cold, clear night.

He wanted to play it like that, without making a single mistake.

"Thank you," he said.

"You're welcome," she said. "Your turn."

They walked over to the magical piano and settled in together, one of them playing without hearing and the other one listening to invisible melodies.

Ben practiced and practiced and practiced, clicking away at keys that were not connected to hammers or strings and could not summon notes.

But as he kept going, a funny thing happened. He started hearing them anyway.

Not with his ears. Not with his brain. But with some other part deep within that he didn't have a name for yet.

Ben looked over at Mrs. Ezra, wondering if she had heard the music, too.

"Yes," she said, nodding with smiling eyes. "You're getting there, Ben. Keep going."

And so he did.

CHAPTER 17

Janet was late again on Wednesday.

But Ben knew better than to point it out. Instead, he said, "Good morning."

Hi, Ben. How's *calculus*?

Janet asked, saying "calculus" the way you might hold the smelly diaper of a baby you just changed.

"It's going *great*," he replied. "I'm pretty sure I'll get a *perfect* score on today's test."

"After studying for *one day*?"

"I practiced *so* much." Ben sensed he was heading into dangerous territory but had no idea how to stop.

"Wow," said Janet. "A perfect score after *just one day.* I'd sure be impressed."

Impressing Janet was a start. "Would you also be . . . *inspired*?"

"What do you mean?"

"To be *more perfect* yourself?"

"Sure, Ben." Janet smirked. "If you get a perfect score on Mr. P.'s impossible test, I will get myself to the corner on time."

Deal,

said Ben, sticking out his hand.

Deal,

said Janet, giving it a firm shake.

Now Ben didn't just *want* to get a perfect score. Now he *had* to.

While Mr. P. talked about irregular spelling, Ben sneaked worried glances at the pages of his calculus book, which rested like an iron slab in his lap. He studied so hard he got a little sweaty. But all the effort didn't help a bit. He wasn't even sure where to start.

Ben had plans to study with Darby at recess, but as he read through the pages, he got so confused that he wanted to scream, shout, and break lightbulbs.

He made up his mind. He *did not* love calculus. There was no use pretending any longer. He would let Darby know and remove it from his list and focus on things he knew he loved for sure.

When recess came, Ben marched straight over to the bench where Darby was sitting.

I have something to tell you,

they both said at the very same time.

"You first," they both said at the same time.

"Go ahead," said Ben.

"Okay," said Darby. "I just want to say how happy I am that you're such a big fan of calculus. I've never met anyone my own age who loves it as much as I do. It just . . . means so much to me." Darby beamed, his eyeballs glistening with gratitude. "Now. What did *you* want to say?"

Ben felt like someone trying to coax a cat back into a bag.

Just that . . . it's amazing that *you* love calculus as much as *I* do!

Darby looked even more delighted now. "Where's your book?" he asked, pointing to Ben's empty hands. "I thought we were going to study for the test."

"Oh . . . I'm feeling so good that I didn't even bring it. I'm 100 percent ready."

"Really?" Darby was excited. "So you understand the tangent-theta-over-two substitution?"

"Well, *of course* I do." Now that Ben had started to dig himself a hole, it was easier to keep going deeper.

"Amazing! And you've learned how to execute the polynomial Euclidean algorithm to break a composite denominator into partial fractions so that every rational function becomes integrable using only logarithms and inverse trigonometric functions?"

"Oh. Yes. *Totally.*"

"*Incredible!* Then you definitely have a special gift."

"What do you mean?"

"I mean, I can't make any promises, but if you learned this much calculus that quickly, it's possible you might be a superhero, too."

Ben knew he had to stop digging, and right away, before he hit the middle of the earth and got burned to a crisp.

I mean, I don't know *everything* about calculus.

But Darby wasn't listening. He looked at Ben with fiery excitement. "Important question! What will your superhero name be? Picking the right name is essential."

"To be honest, I haven't thought—"

Don't worry. I have. How about . . .

BENtastic?

Or, even better . . .

stuBENdous?

Ben liked them both. But neither felt *quite* right. Then he thought of his jersey and had an idea.

How about . . .

the **Big buBENgo?**

 I love it!
said Darby, beaming like
the sun at high noon.

"Me too," said Ben,
allowing himself to step away
from unpleasant reality and
into the beautiful dream. If he
were an actual superhero, he'd
cook the perfect dinner with
a twitch of an eyebrow and
wash his jersey with a flick of
his wrist. Then he'd take Janet
on a flying tour of Honeycutt,
and she would be inspired and
on time, and they could all be
perfect together.

For just that moment, the
life Ben longed for seemed
perfectly within reach.

All he had to do was pull
off the impossible.

When they got back to class, Mr. P. handed out the test. Ben did the first nine problems quickly. And then he came to question number ten.

First Ben tried to solve the problem, but that was like trying to knock down a mountain with a marshmallow.

Next he tried to *just feel it,* but that was like trying to hug a tarantula with a dinosaur head and grizzly bear breath.

Ben considered simply giving up. It had worked with baseball.

But giving up meant crushing Darby's hopes. And missing his chance to inspire Janet. Ben had to live up to his side of the deal.

And so he asked himself, *What would Darby do?*

Ben knew Darby would tell him to do something he truly loved. But neither playing piano nor riding his scooter was helpful at the moment.

What *else* did he enjoy?

Ben liked solving puzzles! And figuring out how to get a perfect score on an impossible test was an extremely tricky puzzle!

But . . . Ben reasoned . . . solving the puzzle didn't require knowing how to calculate the answer. It just meant finding out what the answer *was*.

Ben knew he was in the same *room* as the answer. It was written on Darby's paper, which was on Darby's desk, which was in the corner of the classroom right next to the shelf with the tissues.

It was a classroom rule that as long as you were quiet about it, you could stand up and get a tissue if you really needed to blow your nose.

Since there wasn't enough time to get an actual cold, Ben decided to get a fake one.

He sniffled quietly to see if anyone would notice. No one did. He sniffled *louder.*

Mr. P. glanced up at Ben, who pointed to his nose and then gestured to the tissues, as if to say, *I know we're in the middle of a math test, but would it be okay if I took a moment to blow my nose, since I have an actual cold?*

Mr. P. gave Ben a concerned look and then gestured as if to say, *Of course, Ben. I'm so sorry about your actual cold. Please help yourself to a tissue. And for the record, I'm not at all suspicious of your motives.*

Ben smiled and stood up. He didn't feel great. As he walked toward the back of the classroom, his knees were shaking so badly that he almost fell over.

As he walked back toward his desk, he *almost* forced himself to look the other way so he wouldn't see Darby's answer to the impossible question.

He'd glanced at Darby's paper so quickly that he wasn't even sure if he'd seen the answer correctly, but he made his best guess and wrote it down.

As he grabbed a tissue and pretended to blow his un-runny nose, Ben almost started giggling because he was so nervous and almost started crying because he felt so guilty.

When he got back to his desk, Ben pretty much collapsed into his chair.

The rest of the day was a miserable blur. Ben felt so far from perfect that he spent an hour lying on a cot in the nurse's office, certain he had come down with something much worse than a cold.

CHAPTER 18

On Thursday morning, Ben had a runny nose.
A real one.

His mom didn't burn the pancakes, but Ben
couldn't taste them. Dumbles gave him seven
cuddles and eleven licks, but Ben hardly noticed.
He was sick in his body and also in his heart and
couldn't tell which hurt worse.

When he got to the corner with the yellow bush a few minutes late, Janet was already there.

"Surprise!"

"Wow," said Ben. It was even more shocking than the time Dumbles had coughed up a golf ball.

Here I am,

said Janet with a gallant bow.

"But . . . we don't even know if I got a perfect score yet."

"That's true," she said, "but I'm proud of you already."

"You *are*?"

Janet's words hurt like a booster shot you weren't expecting.

SURPRISE!

"I am. You inspired me, Ben. Not by being perfect, but for caring enough to try. And so here I am, on time."

Wow, said Ben, wanting to appreciate the moment but also feeling like he'd swallowed a pinecone.

You look like you swallowed a pinecone, said Janet with a forehead full of worried wrinkles.

Are you okay?

Just a little under the weather, said Ben, pointing to his stuffy nose as if it were the actual problem.

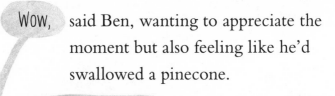

Ready to go?

Yes. And look! We have plenty of time to walk nice and slow so we won't get all sweaty.

Great,

said Ben.

Perfect.

And it should have been. Instead, it felt like Opposite Day and the end of the world all in one.

CHAPTER 19

"Exciting news!" said Mr. P. "I've already graded the most recent math test, and we have *another* perfect score."

Ben was relieved! Mr. P. had said "score" instead of "scores," which meant Ben *hadn't* written down Darby's answer correctly. Which meant he *hadn't* actually cheated.

"Congratulations, Darby, for once again doing what I thought was truly impossible. *Excellent* work."

Kyle groaned. Darby said nothing. Janet gave Ben a sympathetic smile.

Mr. P. started a new lesson, but Ben couldn't hear what it was. He had never been happier to have messed something up. A tiny imperfection had saved him from a big one that might have

The recess bell rang.
Ben put on his jacket and was
about to walk out the door when
Mr. P. tapped him on the shoulder.

May I see you for a moment, Ben?

His voice was steady and calm,
the opposite of the voice a teacher
would use if he thought you had
cheated on a math test.

Ben's brain fought the prickly
sensation that was worming its way
through his insides, from his forehead
to the tips of his toes. He promised
himself that everything was going to
be okay.

The other kids left, and it was just Ben and Mr. P. standing there, both of them waiting for the other to speak. But Ben held on to his silence like the ocean holds on to a shipwreck.

So Mr. P. went first. "Why did I ask you to stay behind, Ben?"

You like my sweater and wonder where I got it?

Nope.

You want to know how I feel about the new bulletin board?

Mr. P. shook his head. His expression was as blank as a brand-new notebook.

I wanted to talk about calculus. I had no idea you were so good at it.

Ben started digging again. "That's recent."

"Oh?"

"Darby has been teaching me."

"I see. That must be why you both got the correct answer on question number ten."

I got it *right?*

Ben felt
panicked
and
confused.

I thought you said only
Darby got a perfect score.

"Darby is the only one who answered *all ten* questions correctly. You missed number three."

Mr. P. handed Ben his test sheet. The top said *9/10*. Ben looked at number three in disbelief. *He had forgotten to carry the two!*

"So that's why you wanted to talk to me? Because I missed such an easy question?"

"No, Ben, I wanted to talk about question number ten. I'd love to hear how you arrived at the answer."

Ben felt like a bone about to break. Like a branch about to snap. Like an egg that had just rolled off the counter and was heading toward the floor. There was just one way to stop the falling.

I looked at Darby's test.

The words were a blade that cut right through the lie. Ben felt terrified but also relieved.

Why, Ben?

asked Mr. P. like it actually hurt.

Because . . . I'm trying to be perfect.

Mr. P. softened a little.

Why is that?

Ben took out his fortune and handed it to his teacher.

Or at least as *more perfect* as I can possibly be.

Mr. P. nodded.

I see.

He handed the fortune back to
Ben and leaned against his desk.

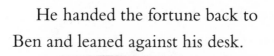

Do you know why I put one
impossible question on every test?

No. Ben had always
wondered.

Why?

So that no one gets a perfect
score. And no one *expects* to.

But Darby did.

"Yes!" said Mr. P., shaking his head
like he still couldn't believe it. "Darby has
a special mind when it comes to math.
I'm going to have to figure out a way to
make my tests even *more* difficult."

"I'm going to keep practicing until I
get a perfect score, too," Ben promised.
"If Darby can do it, then I—"

"I'm going to make sure that never happens," Mr. P. interrupted.

"Why?"

"Because getting a perfect score might make you think you know everything. Which you absolutely don't, and never will."

"But what if someone *does*?"

"Sorry, but no one does. Not Darby. Not even I do. Which is exactly how it should be."

Ben was utterly confused, and his face must have shown it.

Mr. P. leaned in, his eyes soft and kind.

Can I tell you a secret?

Ben nodded
and hoped for the best.

"It's *possible* that a long time ago, a young Titus Piscarelli borrowed someone else's answer."

No!

"When I was in fifth grade. I sat behind Belinda Hodgkins and copied her answers on a math test."

Why?

"Because my parents told me that if I got an A, they'd let me spend the weekend with my uncle in New York."

Ben was thrilled. *Mr. P. understood!* "Did you get caught?"

"Oh yes. Here's a thing to know, Ben. Cheaters *always* get caught."

What happened to you?

"A kind and understanding teacher gave me a second chance. On one condition."

What was it?

Ben sensed he might be given a second chance, too, but wondered how much it was going to hurt.

"From that moment on, I had to be *perfect*."

"But you said—"

"In this one small way, you *have* to be. Perfectly honest. Perfectly responsible for doing your own work. Perfectly willing to accept when you don't know the answer. Got it?"

"*Got* it."

"All right, then," said Mr. P. "Welcome to your second chance. As for this test . . ." Mr. P. took out a fat red marker and wrote *0/10—F.*

"But I got eight problems right!"

Mr. P. gave Ben a look like a broken window gives a baseball.

Ben knew he didn't and shook his head to show it.

Mr. P. handed him the paper. "Do you truly want to be . . . *more perfect*?"

Ben nodded.

"Then pay attention when you make mistakes. Each one is a rung on a ladder."

"To where?"

"To the most perfect version of yourself."

Ben liked the sound of that, but he wanted to know how long it would take. "How tall is the ladder?"

"I don't know," said Mr. P. with a kind smile. "I'll let you know if I ever get to the top."

Ben folded the paper and slid it into his pocket.

He felt bad. He felt good.

He felt ready to climb.

CHAPTER 20

There were still a few minutes of recess left. Ben walked over to the bench and sat down next to Darby.

"Not quite perfect at calculus yet?" asked Darby, who seemed disappointed but not entirely surprised.

"Not *quite*," said Ben, who didn't see any reason to dig into the details. "But getting closer, I think." He *really* didn't want to talk about calculus.

How's it going with "Clair de lune"?

Making progress.

But still not perfect?

Not yet.

Darby seemed even more disappointed. Ben wanted to make him proud.

"Well, that brings us to the Chute," said Darby. "Have you been picturing it?"

Ben hadn't. He'd been so focused on baseball and calculus and Janet and pancakes that he hadn't thought about the Chute at all. He *wanted* to tell Darby he'd been picturing it constantly, that Darby was an excellent teacher, and that Ben was well on his way to perfection. But he couldn't stomach the thought of lying again, not after his promise to Mr. P.

So Ben closed his eyes and pictured himself barreling down the Chute on his scooter,

somehow surviving both jumps, just barely making it around the hairpin turn, and not quite wiping out in the gravel before . . .

smashing right into Dead Man's Tree!

Ben's eyes flashed open in fear.

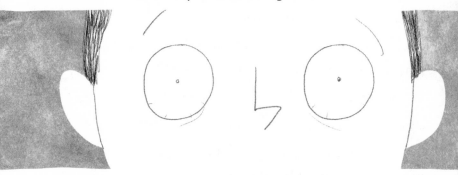

There was Darby, waiting
wide-eyed for an answer.

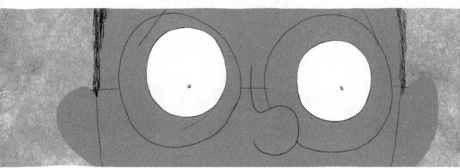

"Yep, I *have* been picturing it," said Ben.
"Recently, in fact."

"Great! And do you finally *believe* you can do
it?" Darby looked at Ben like a chemist looks into
her microscope. It was so clear what he wanted to
hear that Ben tried to meet him halfway.

"I believe it more than I did before." *Which
was true!* Before, he hadn't believed at all, and
now he believed at least a little.

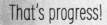

That's progress!

said Darby, grabbing both of Ben's
shoulders and staring straight into his soul.

In that case, I think
you should just *do* it.

I should?

Absolutely. Seize the momentum
before it fades away. I believe in you,
Ben. Do you believe in yourself?

Darby spoke with the same sort of fiery gleam
Coach Stout got when he was giving the team a
pep talk.

"I . . . I do, but—"

"Then show me that you mean it! Run
the Chute!" Darby was so excited he was
practically shouting.

Just then, the kickball skidded across the grass
and bumped into Ben's leg. And then there was
Janet, rushing to get it. She was bright red and
breathless and sweaty. And *mad*.

What did you say?

She tore into
Darby like lightning
striking the tallest
tree in the forest.

Darby glared back. "I wasn't talking to you."

"Well, I'm *definitely* talking to you, and I'm telling you to stop messing up Ben's life."

"*Excuse* me?" Darby stood up and straightened his back, seeming taller and stronger, even with his glasses still on.

But Janet wasn't backing down. "You heard me."

"Since you seem to have been eavesdropping on our *private* conversation, then you probably also heard me say that I believe in Ben, which is the exact *opposite* of messing up his life."

"You sure have a strange way of showing it."

"What are you talking about?"

It's one thing that you tricked Ben into quitting baseball. And that you convinced him to waste his time on math we're not even supposed to learn until high school.

But if Ben gets hurt because you pressure him into running the Chute, I will use my imperfect left foot to kick your perfect behind.

A few kids had gathered nearby, having noticed that something more interesting than kickball was happening.

I do believe in Ben, said Darby.

I believe in him, too.

Then let him make his own decisions.

Fine. But first, I'd like to ask you a question.

Fire away.

I assume you'd never ask Ben to do something you wouldn't do yourself?

Darby's eyes grew wide with indignation, but he held his ground.

Of course not.

So you'd run the Chute first?

Darby and Janet glared at each other like two moose getting ready to bash their antlers together. More and more kids were gathering now, forming a circle around them. Everyone leaned in a little, eager to hear how Darby would respond to Janet's challenge.

"I would . . . ," said Darby, channeling the strength of Darbino for just a moment before settling back into his regular self, like a shaken soda suddenly bubbling up before dying back down again. "But . . . as I told you before, I only do things that interest me."

Janet sensed weakness and pounced.

"Ben believes in me," Darby replied. "He doesn't need proof. Right, Ben?"

Ben *wanted* to jump in and defend his friend, but he let himself pause just a moment too long.

While Ben waffled, Janet stormed on.

"Before Ben risks his life running the Chute, I'm pretty sure he'd want to know whether you're as perfect as you claim. Wouldn't *all of you* like to know?" Janet asked, looking out at the crowd.

Run the Chute!

Kyle shouted.

Run the Chute!

echoed Lang.

As other kids joined in, Darby's face grew ashen and bleak, like a forest after a fire.

Ben felt like the rope in a tug-of-war, stretched tight between two warring giants, neither one willing to give an inch.

Darby had asked Ben to have faith in him, and Ben had tried. But ever since he'd started following Darby's advice, his life had gotten *worse*. Ben was willing to be patient, but only if perfection was actually *possible*.

"Yes," said Ben, thinking maybe he could have it both ways. "I *would* like to see Darby run the Chute. But only because it would give you—*all of you*—a chance to see how amazing he is."

"Stop it, Ben," Darby pleaded, more desperate now than angry.

"But this is the perfect opportunity to show everyone what you're capable of!" Ben insisted.

"It's just that . . ." For the first time since Ben had known him, Darby seemed unsure of what to say next.

"What's wrong?"

I . . .

I actually don't know if I can do it.

Darby slumped. Janet smirked. The crowd grew hushed. Ben could hardly believe what was happening. It was like watching Superman, helpless and paralyzed by a hunk of glowing Kryptonite, unable to summon the strength he needed to save the day—or even himself.

Kyle started to snicker, and Lang was right behind him. Each passing moment made Darby seem weaker and smaller and further from his perfect self.

One thing was clear. Darby needed rescuing. It was time for the Big Bu*BEN*go to step in.

Ben turned to look at the circle of kids. "There's more to Darby than any of you realize. He's not just great at math. He can do amazing flips. He can play kickball better than any of you. And he can run the Chute. He can do anything he wants to do *perfectly* because he's actually . . ."

But Ben stopped. The one thing everyone needed to hear was the one thing he wasn't allowed to say.

"Actually *what*?" said Janet.

Ben needed some help. "Come *on*, Darby," Ben pleaded. "*Show* them!"

But Darby just stood there, stunned and silent.

"Show us what?" Kyle taunted. "How to do math? Or"—he turned to make sure everyone was listening—"how to be *boring*?"

It was the final straw. If Darby lacked the strength to show everyone how incredible he was, then Ben would do it for him.

"What you guys don't realize is that Darby is actually"—Ben reached over, pulled off Darby's glasses, and held them high above his head—

A SUPER-HERO!

Ben held his breath as he waited for Darbino to rise up majestically and save the day.

But it didn't happen.

Instead of a "Thank you," Ben got a withering look of betrayal as Darby snatched his glasses and put them back on.

Instead of enthusiastic cheers, Ben heard laughter and snickering chatter as the whole school pointed and Darby collapsed like a building that suddenly lost all its nails.

Oh, Ben,

said Janet with a complicated expression that was half pity and half amusement.

You don't *actually* think Darby is a . . . ? I mean . . . *really?*

Ben felt the hot, prickly flush of embarrassment and shame. He realized all at once that he'd gotten carried away.

"What's wrong, Super Darby?" said Kyle with a mocking sneer. "Did you lose your mask?"

"Stop it," Ben pleaded. "Stop it, all of you." But no one was listening. Not even Janet. He'd started a fire, and as loud as he shouted, he couldn't put it out.

"I'll do it," said Darby, coming back to life suddenly, like someone waking up from a very bad dream.

"What?" Ben wondered if he'd heard correctly.

"I said, I'll do it," Darby repeated, louder this time, walking over to Janet, standing straight, and looking like Darbino again.

Name the time.

The crowd fell silent. Every ear was hungry for the next bite of excitement.

"This afternoon," said Janet. "Four-thirty sharp. Bring your own snacks."

You'll regret this,

said Darby, glaring at Janet like a soaring hawk glares at a field mouse.

Not as much as you will,

said Janet with a smug grin that made her look like someone Ben had never met and didn't really want to know.

The bell rang. Recess was over.

"Come on, Ben," said Janet, gloating like she'd already won the war. But Ben took one look at Darby's face and saw he had a different battle ahead.

"Give me a second."

Janet gave Ben a *Whatever* look and headed back inside.

Ben walked over to where Darby was standing with his hands in his pockets, gazing toward the hills beyond the schoolyard. He didn't know where to start.

But Darby did.

"I asked you to believe in me," said Darby, so furious he was practically spitting the words.

"I do believe in you! That's why I wanted everyone to see how great you are."

"You have it all backward," said Darby. "Believing in someone doesn't mean forcing them to prove themself!"

Darby's anger was like the blast of scorching heat when you open the oven. Ben wanted to shut the door again quick, to make everything right.

"I'm so sorry," said Ben. "I can't wait to see you run the Chute. Then I'll know for sure that I can do it, too."

Darby looked at Ben with eyes that were empty and unapologetic, like Batman's when he destroys your suburban home in order to save the entire city.

"If you need to see me run the Chute to believe in yourself, I'll do it. If you need other people to believe I'm perfect before you're willing to believe it yourself, that's fine, too. But our lessons are over."

Ben's heart grew as heavy as lead. "What do you mean?"

I'VE FALLEN, AND I CAN'T GET UP!

"You're just like my friend Glenn from my old school. He told everyone about Darbino, too."

"Is *that* why you left the academy?"

Darby nodded. "Once people know Bruce Wayne is Batman, it's over. His powers are basically gone. I came to Honeycutt for a fresh start, and it was awful at first, but then I met you, and let myself believe that things would be different. Because I thought *you* were different."

"I am," Ben insisted, wanting so badly for it to be true. "How can I convince you?"

"Can you give me back my secret?"

Ben saw the problem.
He searched for the words
that would make everything
okay again, but they were somewhere
far away, and he was stuck right there.
As much as he loved solving
puzzles, this was a knot
he couldn't untangle.

I didn't think so,

said Darby, giving Ben one
final disappointed look before
straightening his invisible cape
and walking back inside.

CHAPTER 21

After school, Ben walked home with Janet.

"We sure showed him," she said, skipping excitedly along the sidewalk.

Ben was too sad to walk fast.

"What's wrong with you?" Janet slowed down and looked at Ben like a mom looks at a kid who isn't eating his ice cream.

"Darby is my friend."

Ugh, said Janet.

Can't you see he's a total fake?

"He's not!" said Ben, wondering what he actually believed.

Nothing made sense. Ben needed something to hold on to. He reached into his pocket to find his fortune.

When he did, something else fell out.
A piece of folded paper.

Janet scooped it up and was just about
to hand it to Ben when a look of confusion
and disbelief flashed across her face. "Zero
out of ten on your math test? I don't
understand."

Every part of Ben stopped
working all at once. He
forgot how to breathe.
He couldn't hear or
smell or even feel his
fingers. His whole
body was numb
and stuck like
someone trapped
inside a block of
ice adrift in outer
space.

"Explain this, Ben," Janet demanded with
growing rage. "I have a theory that can't possibly
be true."

Ben didn't speak. He couldn't.

"What did you do?"

But Janet already knew.

I messed up, Ben admitted. I was trying to be perfect.

"NO!" Janet was a bonfire. "Cheating doesn't make you perfect, Ben. It makes you a liar! Tell me this. Did you *ever* love calculus? Did you *ever* understand it? Was there *ever* a chance you were going to get a perfect score on that test?"

"No," Ben admitted. "No to all of it."

Janet got right up in his face. "What is the one thing I asked of you, Ben? The one thing?"

Ben knew what the one thing was. "To never lie to you."

"To never lie to me! When I pick a best friend, I expect results."

Ben knew Janet deserved better. "I'm sorry. I swear it won't happen again."

"It certainly won't," said Janet as she turned and started marching angrily down the sidewalk. "Because I'm not going to let it."

Ben tried to keep up, but he was all out of steam. Out of arguments and excuses. Out of ways to say sorry.

He watched until she got to the corner with the yellow bush, turned left, and stormed angrily away.

Ben stood there for a while, wanting to follow but knowing that the road was closed, maybe forever.

CHAPTER 22

Ben walked home. His parents wouldn't be back from work for a few hours, so he expected the house to be empty.

But someone was there. It was Aunt Nora. She was sitting at Ben's dad's computer, quietly crying and staring at the screen.

Ben forgot all about his own problems and ran over to give her a hug.

What's wrong?

Nora was tough. She was not a crier. Ben had
a theory about who could be enough of a jerk to
make Nora cry.

"Cuonzo?"

"Cuonzo." Nora sniffled and tried to smile
but couldn't quite get there. She dabbed the sides
of her eyes with a tissue.

Cuonzo was Nora's latest boyfriend. He drove
a loud car with no roof and unusual hubcaps.

"I'm sorry," said Ben. "Want me to make you
a sandwich?" Ben made a mean PB&J.
That did the trick. Nora smiled, and
when she did, Ben felt better himself.

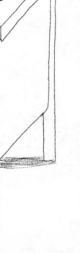

"No thanks," she said. "I
couldn't eat if I tried."

"What are you doing here?"

"I'm applying for a job. Your
dad said I could use his computer."

"Sounds good," said Ben. He
thought about making himself a
PB&J, but suddenly the idea of
walking all the way to the kitchen
was just too much.

215

Instead, he collapsed into the couch and, without really trying, gave the longest, deepest, saddest sigh.

Nora came over and sat next to him, so close that their knees were almost touching. She took his hand and gave it a squeeze. "Speak, nephew. What's going on?"

Ben wasn't sure where to start. In his quest to be perfect, he had messed up pretty much everything.

Let me ask it a different way,

said Nora.

How do you *feel?*

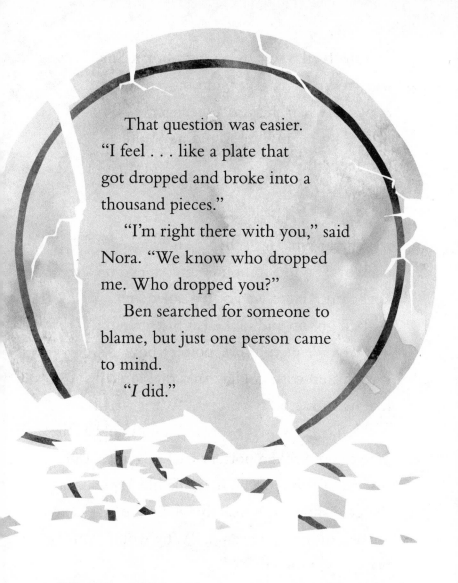

That question was easier.
"I feel . . . like a plate that
got dropped and broke into a
thousand pieces."

"I'm right there with you," said
Nora. "We know who dropped
me. Who dropped you?"

Ben searched for someone to
blame, but just one person came
to mind.

"*I* did."

"Yeah," said Nora, letting out a great big sigh
of her own. "I've been there. This is a thing that
people do."

Ben managed the smallest smile.

"You know what Oba Reiko would do?"

Oba Reiko was his grandmother. She had grown up in Japan and moved to America when she was a teenager. She was wise and fierce and not quite five feet tall.

"What?"

Nora made a forgetful face. "I can't remember what it's called." She walked back over to the computer and tapped on the keyboard. "Here we go. It's called *kintsugi*."

Ben got up and looked at the screen. There was a picture of a pottery bowl crisscrossed with golden lines that looked like lightning bolts or scars. "What is it?"

"Kintsugi is an art form that uses gold as the glue to put broken pottery back together. But instead of trying to be invisible like regular glue, the gold shows you exactly where the cracks are."

Ben didn't understand. "Why would you want to see the cracks?"

"To remind you that the bowl was once broken. That it isn't perfect."

"Can't you just *remember* that you broke the bowl and hide the cracks so it looks like it's fixed?"

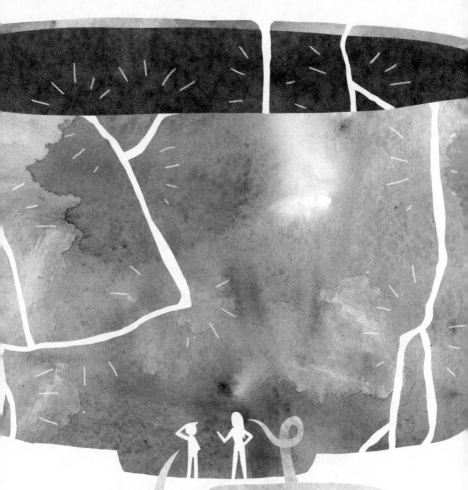

Hiding the cracks doesn't make them go away, Ben.

But why would you want to draw attention to them?

Drawing attention to them is the whole point. If you fill your cracks with gold, you're saying, "Look, this bowl was broken, but I did the hard work of putting it back together, and now it's even stronger than it was before."

Ben thought about that. It was Batman's broken heart that made him so tough and determined to do good for others. Maybe the golden cracks were like his tragic backstory. It wasn't just practice that made him so great. It was never forgetting his imperfection.

Ben reached into his pocket for his fortune, but his fingers found his math test instead. He pulled it out and stared at the paper: *0/10*. The grade was written in red instead of gold, but the message was the same. He had broken something, but now he had a chance to fix it.

Maybe he'd been looking at everything backward. "Would you say the gold makes the bowl *more perfect* than it was before?"

Nora smiled. "I think the gold reminds us that the bowl is perfectly *im*perfect. That even though someone managed to put it back together, it's always going to be a little bit broken, just like the rest of us."

"That makes sense," said Ben, who was more than ready to be put back together. "But where do I find the gold?"

Nora gave him a loving smile that was the opposite of the sassy ones she usually preferred. "The gold comes second, Benny. You have to start by picking up the pieces."

That made sense, but the broken bits of Ben's life were hopelessly scattered.

How do I do that?

"One at a time." Nora reached over and gave Ben a hug. "And in my experience, you might want to pick them up carefully. The edges can be sharp."

Ben thought about Janet. And Darby. And Coach Stout. So many people were mad at him.

At that moment, Ben didn't feel like doing the hard, sharp work of putting things back together. He wanted to just sit there with someone as perfectly imperfect as he was.

Nora seemed to feel the same way.

And so they stopped talking and wrapped their arms around each other like tangled strips of golden glue, doing their best to hold the world together.

CHAPTER 23

The phone rang. It rang again.

It might have been Ben's mom asking him to take the pork chops out of the freezer. Or it might have been his dad asking what kind of tacos he wanted for dinner. Or . . . it could be his gold. That thrilling possibility gave Ben the lift he needed to walk across the room and pick up the phone.

Hello?

Please come immediately. I have a problem that only you can solve.

Ben knew from the voice that it was Mrs. Ezra, even though she didn't say so.

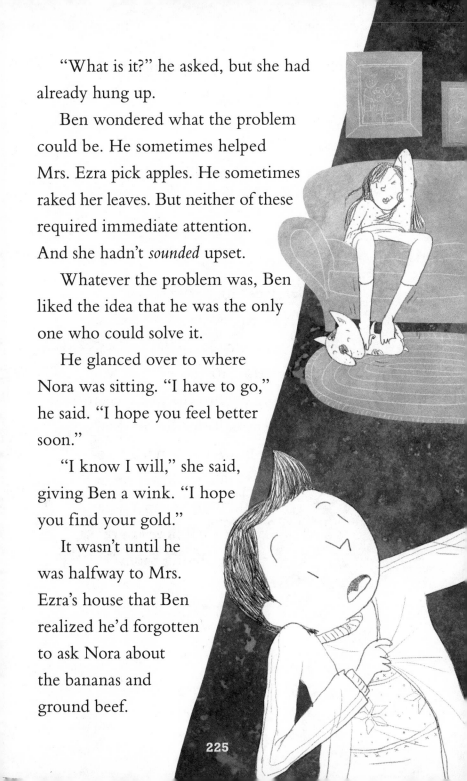

"What is it?" he asked, but she had already hung up.

Ben wondered what the problem could be. He sometimes helped Mrs. Ezra pick apples. He sometimes raked her leaves. But neither of these required immediate attention. And she hadn't *sounded* upset.

Whatever the problem was, Ben liked the idea that he was the only one who could solve it.

He glanced over to where Nora was sitting. "I have to go," he said. "I hope you feel better soon."

"I know I will," she said, giving Ben a wink. "I hope you find your gold."

It wasn't until he was halfway to Mrs. Ezra's house that Ben realized he'd forgotten to ask Nora about the bananas and ground beef.

He climbed onto Mrs. Ezra's porch and knocked on her door, which opened almost immediately.

"I'm so glad you could make it," she said. "Come in. Come in!"

Ben went in. Felicity yipped as she ran in excited circles. "There's no time to waste," said Mrs. Ezra, walking over to the table where she kept her goldfish, Brenda. She lifted the bowl and handed it to Ben. "If you don't mind, Brenda would prefer to spend her final hours in the living room."

Oh no,

said Ben, taking the bowl.

Is she . . . *dying?*

"Who knows? Goldfish tend not to live very long. Which means we have to live this day as if it were her last."

Ben didn't have time to point out that Brenda looked perfectly healthy to him, because Mrs. Ezra had already opened the door to the living room and was excitedly gesturing for him to follow.

Brenda's bowl was surprisingly heavy. And incredibly full. It was impossible to walk without sloshing a little.

"No sloshing!" said Mrs. Ezra cheerfully.

In order to not slosh, Ben had to keep his eyes locked on the lip of the bowl. Which made it hard to see where he was going.

Right this way,

said Mrs. Ezra, guiding Ben through the door.

You're almost there.

And then she paused for a moment and said,

You're doing such a fine job, dear.

"Are you talking to me?" asked Ben. Mrs. Ezra never called him "dear."

"No, Ben, I was talking to *her*."

"To Brenda?"

"No, Ben. Brenda is a *goldfish*. I was talking to *Janet*."

At the sound of Janet's name, Ben looked up and sloshed.

There she was, right across the room, holding another goldfish bowl, with a big wet slosh mark on her shirt.

They stood there staring at each other, stunned and wet and trying not to slosh, with aching arms and puzzled expressions, as their baffled brains struggled to make sense of things.

> Well, now. Thank you both for coming so quickly. In case you were wondering, Ben, you are the problem I have.

Mrs. Ezra gave Ben a scolding look.

> And you are, too,

she said, lowering her eyebrows at Janet.

"I was driving back from my weekly appointment with my personal trainer when I observed two young people making a ruckus on the street. I found it impossible to tolerate."

Ben didn't know what to say.

But Janet did. "If we're the problem, why did you ask us to come over?"

"Because," said Mrs. Ezra, as bright and excited as a toddler's talking teddy bear, "you are also the *solution*."

"We are?" Ben asked.

Oh yes. Just like four is the solution to *What is two plus two?* Like French silk pie is the solution to a broken heart.

$2 + 2 = 4$

Ben made a mental note to tell Nora.

"You two have some talking to do," Mrs. Ezra continued. "You are not allowed to put Brenda and Herkimer down until you've worked out your differences."

"Herkimer?"

"Never assume you've met all of my goldfish, Ben," said Mrs. Ezra with a disapproving glare.

Ben might have replied, but he was too afraid of sloshing.

"Now . . . I am going to take a long, relaxing bubble bath, and by the time I'm done, I want those goldfish back on the table and you two putting this together." She reached into a cabinet and pulled out a jigsaw puzzle with a photo of two snuggling bunnies on the front.

Ben had to admit it was pretty cute.

Why a jigsaw puzzle?

asked Janet, who was utterly immune to cuteness.

"It's impossible to do a jigsaw puzzle in the middle of a fight," said Mrs. Ezra. "*Trust* me."

Mrs. Ezra started walking through the door, then turned back abruptly. "And no sloshing!"

She shut the door with such force that Ben sloshed.

And then everything was quiet.

Ben stood there, holding a goldfish bowl and looking at Janet, who was holding a goldfish bowl and looking at him.

Brenda was getting heavier by the second.

I guess we'd better get started,

said Janet.

CHAPTER 24

Ben saw his opportunity.

Now that Janet was holding a goldfish bowl, she couldn't march off in an angry huff. Mrs. Ezra was pretty smart.

"I'm sorry," he said. "I'm *really* sorry."

"I get it," said Janet, who already seemed to have cooled down a little. "And I know you didn't mean to hurt me. It just *felt* like you did."

"Are you going to forgive me?" Ben really wanted to put down the bowl.

"Maybe," said Janet. "I am prepared to forgive my friend Ben."

Ben was confused. He wondered if the pressure of the situation was messing with his ears. "Does that mean you're prepared to forgive . . . *me*?"

"Yes. As long as you and my friend Ben are still the same person. I want Ben back."

"I'm right here." Ben wanted to raise his hands and point to himself, but Brenda was making it impossible.

"Are you sure? Because my friend Ben loves baseball. And he's a little iffy about math. And he would *never* cheat on a test."

"Your friend Ben is trying really hard to be perfect. You said you were proud of me for that."

"Not if it makes you do stupid, un–Ben-like things."

Perfection is a lonely road,

said Ben, hoping it would inspire a little sympathy.

Perfection is ... it's ...

Janet was searching for the perfect word.

It's ... *boring!* Who wants to do everything right all the time? What fun is that?

Ben was desperate to make Janet understand. He needed an example she couldn't possibly deny.

Then, out of the corner of his eye, he saw it. A thing they both loved.

"Look," said Ben, gesturing across the room with his elbow and sloshing a little. "In that bowl. That apple from Mrs. Ezra's tree. You've always said her apples are perfect."

Janet rolled her eyes. "What I mean is that they're extremely tasty. Not that they're actually *perfect*."

"Name one thing that isn't perfect about that apple. It's perfectly red and perfectly shaped and perfectly delicious."

"I'll admit it *looks* perfect," said Janet. "But it could be rotten inside."

Ben was pretty sure it *wasn't*.

"You're impossible," he said.

Ben shuffled over to the table where the apple sat, miraculously not sloshing at all. Then he slowly and carefully bent forward and grabbed the apple with his teeth and took a big, satisfying bite. It was so perfectly delicious that Ben sloshed. A *lot*.

I'm sorry to break it to you,

said Ben, still chewing.

But this apple is definitely perfect.

But . . . according to your definition, the great big bite mark means it *isn't* perfect anymore,

said Janet with a satisfied smirk.

But it used to be!

Ben felt like
he did when he
stepped off a carousel,
and his feet were back on solid
ground but the world kept spinning
anyway. Janet was cheating. He knew
there must be some perfect response.
But at the moment, all the energy
he had left was being used to keep
his grip on Brenda's bowl.

Are you ready to admit
you can't have your perfect
apple and eat it, too?

asked Janet.

Ben was not ready to admit anything of the sort. But he was ready to stop holding Brenda.

"What if we put the bowls down on the table for a minute and keep on trying to work this out?" said Ben.

Good idea, said Janet.

I don't see how Mrs. Ezra would know.

Oh, I'd definitely know, said a voice that wasn't Janet's.

CHAPTER 25

"Mrs. Ezra, is that you?" Janet asked.

"Yes, my dear. I've been eavesdropping. You two are being pretty stubborn."

The door opened, and Mrs. Ezra came in, wearing a bathrobe and a shower cap.

Ben and Janet exchanged worried glances. He had the sense that their goldfish-holding days were far from over.

"Here's what I think," said Mrs. Ezra. "You are both right. And you're both wrong."

"Let's start with how I'm right," said Janet.

"Wonderful," said Mrs. Ezra. "Let's talk about baseball."

What do you know about baseball?

asked Ben in a way that might
have been a little bit rude.

I have forgotten more about baseball
than you will ever know, young man,

Mrs. Ezra snapped.

You have?

Ben couldn't quite believe it.

I *love* baseball, Ben. Do *you*?

Ben wasn't sure how to
answer. He did his best.

I used to . . . before I
realized that I didn't.

Ben *does* love baseball!

said Janet, making
a humongous slosh.

For some reason, he forgot!

"Well, anyone who knows anything about baseball knows that batters usually fail. Even the best players in the world only get a hit about a third of the time."

"Exactly!" said Ben. "That's what makes it so awful."

"No," said Mrs. Ezra. "That's what makes it so *exciting*."

"What do you mean?"

"Baseball is designed to make perfection impossible. It is the *trying* that is beautiful. It is the constant *failing* that makes the game interesting. If everyone had a perfect batting average, baseball would be boring."

YES!

said Janet, like a person who just won a three-foot-tall trophy.

I've been trying to tell him perfection is *boring*.

"But the opposite is also true," said Mrs. Ezra, like a pan that no opinions would stick to. "Ben is right that we are drawn to things that *seem* perfect."

"What do you mean?" asked Janet, like someone whose trophy had just been replaced by a plush giraffe with a bent neck.

Mrs. Ezra walked across the room and turned on her stereo. It took only a few notes before Ben recognized "Clair de lune." He closed his eyes. It sounded like an angel on roller skates gliding across a hilly landscape. Every note was exactly right. The rise and the swell of the music was . . . *perfect*.

The song ended, and Ben opened his eyes. There were tears on Janet's cheeks.

"What do you think?" Mrs. Ezra asked Janet.
"Was it perfect?"

Yes,

said Janet, nodding her
head and wiping her
face on her shoulder.

It absolutely was.

"Was it boring?"

No way.

Mrs. Ezra looked at Ben now.
"What made it perfect?"

Ben didn't even
have to think.

Because whoever
played it didn't make
a single mistake!

Mrs. Ezra frowned. "No, Ben. The absence of mistakes is not what makes that recording perfect. Do you know, Janet?"

Janet shook her head. "Tell us!"

"I won't," said Mrs. Ezra. "Some lessons mean more when you learn them yourself."

Ben and Janet exchanged a glance. For just a second, they were back on the same page, united in not knowing what Mrs. Ezra was up to.

"Let me ask you a different question, Janet. Did whoever played the piano in that recording practice a lot?"

"Definitely."

"Was it worth it?"

"For sure."

Mrs. Ezra looked at Ben now.

"Is it just as worth it for the Big Bubango to practice and practice so he can hit .345?"

"Yes."

"Is he ever going to be perfect?"

"No."

"If he's not perfect, then what is he?"

"He's . . ." Ben searched for words that seemed right. "He's . . . *pretty darn good*?"

Mrs. Ezra made a face like someone who's tasting a new kind of soup and needs a second to realize how delicious it is. "Yes," she said with a twinkle of excitement in her eyes. "I think that's *exactly* right. The Big Bubango is *pretty darn good*."

Mrs. Ezra opened a drawer, took out a thick black marker, and started writing. *Directly on the wall!*

PRACTICE MAKES PERFECT

And then she crossed out "PERFECT" and wrote:

PRACTICE
MAKES ~~PERFECT~~
PRETTY
DARN GOOD.

Ben looked at Janet. Janet looked at Ben.
Mrs. Ezra was nutty in the best possible way.

"Now, here's another question for you, Ben.
Who says perfection is something we should
want in the first place?"

"The fortune!"

"Read it again."

Ben read it again. It was true. The fortune
only said that perfection came from practice. It
didn't say anything about perfection being good.

And yet Ben had a strong sense that perfection was not just good but something he was supposed to want. *Where had that come from?*

Did your parents ever ask you to be perfect?

No.

Did *Janet* ever ask you to be perfect?

Never.

Do they expect you to be pretty darn good?

I think so.

Is that a reasonable request?

Ben thought about that. Were his parents *pretty darn good*? He had to admit they were. Was Janet a *pretty darn good* friend? She was *excellent*!

Yes,

said Ben.

It's *entirely* reasonable.

248

He looked over to see if Janet agreed.

But Janet had the look of someone who has just gotten hit in the face with a snowball. And then the tears began to fall.

I'm so sorry, Ben. First, I got mad at you for wanting to be perfect, and then I got mad at you for not being perfect *enough*. That was unfair and imperfect of me, because you're as pretty darn good as a friend can be.

Ben really didn't want to cry, but Janet's tears were like a great big yawn that makes you need to yawn yourself.

He definitely didn't cry but maybe got a little wet in the face.

I'm sorry I cheated, and I'm even more sorry I lied to you about it, and I'm the most sorry that I made you feel like you had to be perfect. You're already the most perfect friend I could possibly hope for.

Ben wanted to hug Janet, and he was pretty sure that she wanted to hug him. But Brenda and Herkimer were getting in the way.

"Congratulations!" said Mrs. Ezra. "You can put down your goldfish bowls! You are no longer acting ridiculous!"

Ben and Janet put down their bowls. They had a hug. Ben was pretty sure it was the perfect hug, but he wasn't about to say it out loud.

"Now listen up," said Mrs. Ezra like a gym teacher who's not quite ready to give you the ball. "My advice is to surround yourselves with people who are doing their best to be pretty darn good. The more you can find, the better your life will be."

"Okay," said Ben.

"Makes sense," said Janet.

"I'm not done," said Mrs. Ezra, but with her smiling face and not her gym teacher one.

"Be wary of people who think they're perfect.

Because they can't live up to their own

best intentions, they tend to cause

a lot of trouble. And not just for others,

but also for themselves."

Someone should put *that* in a fortune cookie, said Janet.

It might be a *little* too long, said Ben.

"You're probably right," Janet agreed, laughing. Her smile was like the sun coming out after a three-day thunderstorm. But then she made a face like another round of clouds was rolling in.

"What's wrong?" Ben wondered if he needed to get his raincoat.

"If Darby can't live up to his best intentions . . ."

Then there's no way he can run the Chute!

Oh no! said Janet.

What have I done?

Sharing one thought, they looked at the clock on the wall. It was 4:15. It would take at least fifteen minutes to get to the Chute.

Ben's heart lurched with panic. Darby was perfectly well intentioned. But he was about to find himself in a whole lot of trouble.

CHAPTER 26

Ben and Janet hatched a plan. He raced to get his scooter as she sprinted to get her bike. They'd meet at the Chute, and hopefully not too late.

The next stretch of minutes was a blur. Ben rode faster than he ever had. By the time he reached the steep road that led to the top of the Chute, he was already exhausted and needed to stop. Instead, he kept going. It was 4:28. Darby seemed like the kind of person who would do things exactly on time. Even risking his life to prove a point.

When Ben got to the top of the Chute, he had to fight his way through a huge crowd of kids who were there to see Darby attempt the impossible.

Darby!

Ben screamed.

DARBY!!

Through the sea of arms and shoulders and heads, Ben caught a glimpse of Darby, poised on his bike at the edge of the Chute.

DON'T DO IT!

Ben screamed.

YOU DON'T HAVE ANYTHING TO PROVE!

Darby turned and looked at Ben with a face like a bulb that's about to burn out. "Of course I do."

"You don't! Why do you care what they think?"

"I *don't* care what they think."

"Then why are you doing this?"

"I care what *you* think."

"Why?"

Darby shook his head, like he'd finally come up against a problem he didn't know how to solve. "I'm not sure," he admitted, lifting his foot and placing it on the pedal.

And then he turned to Ben with an expression of utter triumph, like the first person to plant a flag on the peak of an undiscovered mountain.

Darby threw back his head and opened his mouth.

My name . . .

He took off his glasses and flung them into the bushes.

is . . .

He popped up his collar and strapped on his helmet.

DARBINO!

And then he pressed down on the pedal
and launched forward into empty air.

Ben's heart plunged. He forced his way through the crowd and rushed to the edge of the Chute.

Darbino hit the first jump and flew through the air. He slid when he landed but didn't tip over. Which was already amazing.

Then he hit the second jump and landed a little bit sideways but somehow regained his balance and kept going.

The booming buzz of shared amazement filled Ben's ears. No one could believe what was happening. Another crowd of kids was gathered at the bottom of the hill, gaping in wonder. Darbino was a tiny raft in a surging sea of astonishment.

Next he hit the hairpin turn, which required incredible strength, sharp instincts, and perfect timing. Again, he almost lost control, but again, somehow, he held on.

Then he plowed through the patch of gravel and started to skid but just barely managed to stay upright.

As he met each new challenge, the crowd grew more excited and the cheering grew louder. Darbino was just as incredible as advertised. Flegg practiced every day and had never made it to the bottom without falling at least once. This was Darbino's first time, and he was making it look almost effortless.

Ben was thrilled. Ben was ashamed. Ben was proud. He saw it and felt it and knew it for sure. Whether or not Darbino was actually perfect, whether or not he was wearing his glasses, he was an amazing human being who Ben felt lucky to call his friend.

"I believe in you!" Ben shouted at the top of his lungs. "Not in Darbino! In you, Darby! In *you*!" He didn't care who else heard. It was the truest thing he'd ever said.

Somehow, Ben's words must have cut their way through the chorus of cheers, because Darby glanced up and smiled at him. For just an instant, their eyes connected, and Ben could tell he was forgiven.

But it was exactly the wrong moment for Darby to look away from the Chute. He barreled into Dead Man's Tree, fell backward off his bike, and slammed his leg into the ground.

As his bike tumbled
end over end to the bottom
of the Chute, a hundred kids
gasped all at once.

Then everything
was way too quiet.

Darby lay crumpled and
motionless, his wrecked
body wrapped like a wet
leaf around the
trunk of Dead
Man's Tree.

Ben didn't think as he pushed his scooter over the lip of the Chute. He barely noticed as he began to plummet, far faster than he'd ever gone before. He felt no fear as he flew over the first jump and then the second. He whipped skillfully around the hairpin turn and slid effortlessly through the patch of gravel.

He skidded expertly to a stop not far from where Darby lay.

Ben hopped off his scooter and knelt beside his friend, hoping and begging for some sign of life. He had the faintest sense of other kids cheering.

But all he could see was Darby.

Don't be dead, he thought.
Just please don't be dead.

"Darby! Darby! Are you okay?" Ben touched his friend's shoulder as gently as he could. "It's Ben. I'm here. It's going to be all right."

At the sound of Ben's voice, Darby opened his eyes and looked up with a wild gaze.

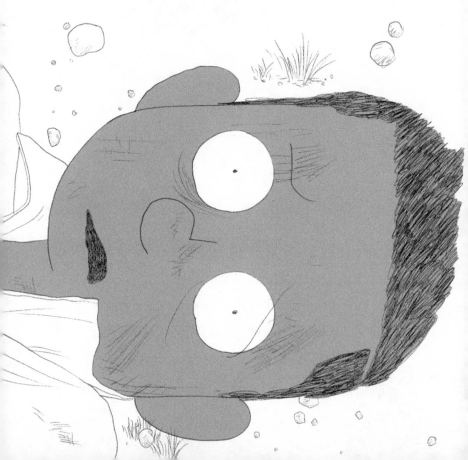

Hi, Ben,

said Darby, not really looking
at Ben but staring into the
sky beyond his head.

That was . . . *amazing.*

Ben took a closer look. Darby's arm was
purple. His leg was bent the wrong way. "We
need to get you to the hospital."

"I've never been to the hospital." Darby spoke
with detached curiosity, as if he couldn't feel the
parts of himself that were broken. It
worried Ben a lot.

"They'll fix you right up." Ben said the things he thought he was supposed to say. "You'll be as good as new."

"I'll be as good as new," Darby echoed, like someone who isn't all the way awake.

Ben looked down the hill. There was Janet, trying her hardest to scramble up. But the Chute was just too steep.

Call an ambulance!

Ben yelled down to her.

And call Darby's parents!

He watched as Janet marched over to a fifth grader named Juniper who spent a lot of time bragging about having a phone.

Ben assumed the best thing was to keep Darby company until the ambulance came. "You did it," he said. "You ran the Chute."

"Not really," said Darby. "Not *perfectly.*"

"You did great," said Ben. "Everyone's amazed."

"I don't care," said Darby. "I told you, I don't."

"Well, *I'm* amazed," said Ben. "You're still perfect as far as I'm concerned."

"No," said Darby, grabbing Ben's arm and staring directly into his eyes, like a plane stares at the runway as it comes in to land.

Can I tell you another secret?

Sure.

Ben leaned in.

Darby closed his eyes and bunched up his forehead like whatever he had to say was going to hurt even worse than his arm and leg. "I'm just Darby. There . . . is no Darbino. I may be good at math and gymnastics, but I'm just a regular kid."

"I know," said Ben, taking Darby's hand and giving it a long, sure squeeze. "That's what I like best about you."

Darby started crying then, which made Ben feel better somehow, because crying made a lot more sense.

A few minutes later, paramedics showed up at the top of the Chute. They scrambled down to where Darby lay and eased him onto a stretcher and then slid him carefully down to the bottom. Ben scrambled down behind them.

At the bottom of the hill, they put Darby onto a cart and pushed him toward the ambulance, which was waiting in a parking lot nearby.

I'm so sorry,

said Janet, running up to Darby as he lay on the stretcher. Her face was a mess of fear and guilt and hope.

This is all my fault. I never should have dared you. I got totally carried away.

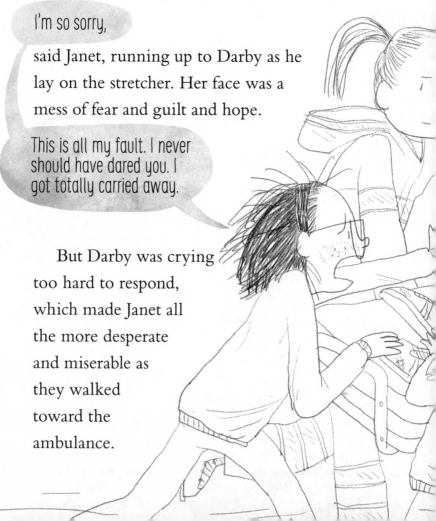

But Darby was crying too hard to respond, which made Janet all the more desperate and miserable as they walked toward the ambulance.

"Step back," said a paramedic as they slid the stretcher inside.

"Can we come with you?" Ben pleaded.

"Are you family?"

"No," said Janet. "He's our *friend*."

Sorry, then no. From the look of his leg, he'll be in the hospital for a few days. Visiting hours are posted online.

"But is he going to be okay?" Ben had to know.

"He's going to be okay," said the paramedic.

He slammed the door, and the ambulance drove off, and Janet burst into tears.

Ben felt pretty darn bad.
Janet looked pretty darn worse.

CHAPTER 27

There was nothing left to say, so Ben and Janet said nothing as they rode back home together.

Janet went to her house, and Ben went to his. It was almost time for dinner, but for maybe the first time in his life, Ben had no appetite. He poked his head into the kitchen, where his mom was cooking something that smelled like headaches.

"I'm going to get some practice in before dinner."

"Sounds good!" she said with a smile. "I love you!"

Ben wondered how she knew that he needed to hear it. No amount of practice seemed to improve her cooking, but the rest of her mom skills were getting better every day.

Ben walked down the block and rang Mrs. Ezra's bell. When she opened the door, he didn't know what to say. It was all too much.

But Mrs. Ezra knew. "I see," she said. "Right this way."

Instead of leading Ben to the magical piano, she pointed to the regular one.

"But I can't," said Ben. He knew he wasn't ready.

"Sit," said Mrs. Ezra. "And play. Just *play*."

Ben sat. He was almost too sad to play. But mostly he was too sad *not* to.

When his fingers pressed the keys and actual notes came out, Ben's sad body filled with joy, from his toenails to his earlobes to the tingling tips of his teeth.

The sound was like a sled gliding with unexpected ease along a smooth and snowy sidewalk. Ben closed his eyes and opened his heart and enjoyed the ride.

He made a few mistakes but didn't stop to stare at them. He rolled forward like forward was down, without a shred of effort, like gravity was helping.

He played like he was flying down the Chute, not stopping to worry whether or not he could make it, because he simply had to.

He played like his brain was not invited. Like his fingers were attached to the necessary rise and fall of his lungs. Like summer wouldn't ever end.

He played with gladness that Janet had forgiven him. He played with relief that Darby wasn't dead. He played from his shadows. He played from his heart.

And then the song ended, and the room was quiet except for the echoes of the last chord fading slowly into stillness.

Well?

Mrs. Ezra looked at Ben like a bee looks at a flower on the first day of spring.

Ben wondered what she meant. She hadn't asked an actual question.

But an answer happened anyway.

"I understand," said Ben, who suddenly knew what he hadn't before. "I know what was perfect about that recording of 'Clair de lune.'"

Mrs. Ezra smiled at Ben like he'd already said the answer, like she already knew it was right. "Tell me."

"It wasn't that there weren't any mistakes."

"Go on."

"It was that . . . the person who played it . . ." Ben *felt* what he wanted to say but didn't know the right words. "He . . . played like he actually *saw* the light of the moon. Like he actually *felt* it."

It was Mrs. Ezra's turn to get watery eyes.

"That is correct. And when you played it just now, you made me see it, too."

"I *did*?"

"That moonlight was so bright I almost had to put on my sunglasses."

Ben smiled. Because he had been right *and* because he had found a way to make moonlight.

"You learn piano with your head, but if you want to play *perfectly,* there comes a terrifying moment when you have to tell your brain to go sit in the corner and play without thinking."

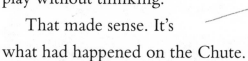

That made sense. It's what had happened on the Chute.

"What you played just now was beautiful, Ben."

"But it wasn't perfect," Ben clarified. "I still made a few mistakes."

"Those weren't mistakes," said Mrs. Ezra. "They were bruises. We get bruises when we're learning anything. Learning to walk. Learning to ride a bike."

"Learning to make pancakes," Ben added.

"Exactly," said Mrs. Ezra. "Or learning to be a good friend. The way you played just now was beautiful . . . with bruises. Which tells me that you're trying. Which means you're living. If we go through life without getting any bruises, we're living pretty small, aren't we?"

Ben thought about that. He wanted to live big.

"Can I play it again?"

"I insist."

Ben rested his fingers on the keys. He closed his eyes. And he played. And played. And played.

He got a few bruises, but not the kind that hurt.

CHAPTER 28

The next morning, the pancakes were pretty darn good.

"Nice job," said Ben in a way that showed he really meant it.

"Thanks!" said his mom in a way that showed she knew it and was proud. "I've been practicing!"

As they stood there and smiled, Ben knew it was time to put down the other goldfish bowl he'd been carrying all week. The one filled up with stubbornness and pride. "I'm sorry," he said, sloshing a little.

"For what?" asked his mom in a way that showed she knew the answer but needed to hear it anyway.

"For being such a jerk the other night."

"That's okay," she said, bending down to look

Ben straight in the eye. "You were right. Those pancakes were terrible."

"Maybe, but—"

"How about this? If you agree to put up with my terrible cooking, I'll do my best to keep an eye on your dad's lip balm situation."

Ben smiled. "That sounds like a fair trade."

She pulled him in and gave him a hug.

"Just promise me one thing."

"Anything." Whatever it was, Ben would give it his best.

"Promise you'll never be perfect."

"Why?" Ben didn't understand. Even though he was done with *trying* to be perfect, he still wouldn't mind if it happened accidentally.

She smiled and placed her hands gently on his shoulders. "Because if you were already perfect, I'd be out of a job."

Ben thought about that. She was right. "I promise to keep you good and busy."

"And I will do the same," she said. "How about you start by clearing your plate?"

Ben got to the corner first. Janet showed up
not long after.

"Good morning," said Ben, who had decided he'd
never again complain about what time she got there.

I'm only seventeen seconds late,

she said in a way that let
Ben know how pleased she
was to see her hard work
paying off.

That's pretty darn good,

said Ben.

I like to think so,

she said with a smile.

School was the same as ever. In social studies, Janet raised her hand.

"Yes?" said Mr. P.

"I've been thinking. It might have been better if the Founding Fathers had written that people should try their hardest to make a *pretty darn good* country instead of a *more perfect* one."

"I take your point, Janet," said Mr. P. "I wish you had been there to suggest it."

We the People
OF THE UNITED STATES
IN ORDER TO FORM A
Pretty darn good
~~MORE PERFECT~~ UNION,
ESTABLISH JUSTICE, INSURE
DOMESTIC TRANQUILITY... etc.

Ben wondered how things might have turned out differently if, in addition to a bunch of Founding Fathers, America could have had at least one Founding Janet. Darby wasn't at school, of course, but he was pretty much the only thing Ben thought about all day.

After school, Janet's mom drove Ben and Janet to the hospital. Ben's heart was a leaking bucket of dread, and Janet's face was covered with something that looked like it hurt even worse.

They checked in at the front desk, and a nurse led them up to Darby's room. Ben knocked, and a moment later, Darby's dad came to the door with a face that was tired and worried. He took one look at Ben, and the worry turned to anger. "I think you should leave."

"Okay," said Ben, happy to have an excuse to escape.

"Wait," said Janet with a face like a sinkhole that's just getting started. "Don't be mad at Ben. I'm the one who dared Darby to ride the Chute. This is all my fault."

"Who are you?" asked Darby's dad, squinting at Janet like the puzzle she was.

"I'm Janet. I have strong opinions and tend to get carried away."

"Then *both* of you should leave. Darby needs his rest."

I'm awake! shouted Darby from inside the room.

Let them in, Dad!

"You need your rest." Darby's dad wasn't going to budge.

Darby's mom came to the door and gently but firmly opened it the rest of the way.

Hi, Ben. Nice to meet you, Janet,

she said with a delicate smile.

Please come in. We were just about to sign Darby's cast.

Darby's dad made a face like a blister that's ready to pop, but he kept the rest of his thoughts to himself as Darby's mom led Ben and Janet into the room.

Darby was flat on his back in a hospital bed. His left leg was in a cast and his left arm was in a splint and he had a brace around his neck.

"Wow," said Janet. She was right about that.

"Hi, Darby," said Ben. "How do you feel?"

"I'm okay," said Darby with a smile that made Ben's insides feel slightly less disorganized.

I'm so sorry, said Janet.

It's okay. Darby wasn't mad at all, which was puzzling.

"No, you don't understand," she insisted. "I'm really, really, really, really sorry."

"Stop it," said Darby. "*I'm* the one who decided to ride down that hill. It might not have been the greatest decision, but it was definitely mine."

"I don't accept that," Darby's dad cut in. "You've always had excellent judgment. You never did foolish things before meeting Ben and Janet. You've always been absolutely—"

"I'm *not,* Dad."

"You're not *what?*"

Everyone knew. But nobody wanted to say.

I'm not *perfect.*

The word shook the room like a mighty gong, rattling everyone into a stretch of uncomfortable silence.

Darby's dad found his words first. "Of *course* you are, son."

"Look at me, Dad." Darby's eyes were pleading. "I'm broken in so many ways. I'm the *opposite* of perfect."

"That's temporary. In a few weeks—"

But Darby didn't want to hear it. "*I'm not perfect!* I've always tried to get as close as I could, but now I know I'm really not. And I don't even *want* to be."

In that moment, Ben saw it, bright and clear, like a flashback in a movie.

Darbino's tragic backstory wasn't about an alien space ray

or a tub of toxic goo.

It was about a boy trying so hard to make his father proud that a superhero was born.

What do you mean?

asked Darby's dad with the breathless expression of someone who's been suddenly punched.

I mean . . . I had fun on that hill!

Darby's eyes were dancing.

You broke your leg!

Okay, but before that, I was . . . flying. I was . . . free. I found something I love.

You love calculus.

I *do* love calculus. I love it because there's always an answer. I loved riding the Chute because . . . there *wasn't* an answer. Anything could have happened.

And look what *did* happen!

287

Darby's dad was begging, almost.

Calculus is safe, Darby.
Calculus makes sense.

"Calculus happens on paper," said Darby's mom gently, as if she were threading a needle while rocking a baby to sleep. "The world isn't always safe and often doesn't make sense."

"And that's why we have to protect him."

No, Charles. It's why he has to get ready. And you don't learn by doing everything right all the time. You learn from messing up. And then trying again and messing up better the next time.

Darby's dad had run out of words, so Darby's mom continued.

"Look," she said. "Look at our son. With his *friends*. His leg might be broken, but he has a *smile* on his face. An actual *smile*."

Darby made a smile so unstoppable and true, it was impossible to not smile back. Even his dad did, just a little.

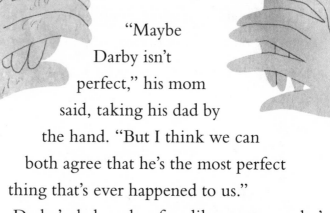

"Maybe
Darby isn't
perfect," his mom
said, taking his dad by
the hand. "But I think we can
both agree that he's the most perfect
thing that's ever happened to us."

Darby's dad made a face like a person who's
trying to say seven things at once but is stuck
having only one mouth. He took a long, deep
breath and let it whisper out slowly, and as it
did, something inside him started to defrost.
He looked at Darby's mom and nodded softly.

Then he reached out and took her hand and
Darby's so the three of them formed a triangle.

Ben decided it was time to spend a few minutes looking out the window at the parking lot, and Janet decided to join him. But they couldn't help listening as Darby's dad began to speak.

I'll tell you this. You've been the perfect son. I can't believe you almost . . .

There were sounds like people doing a terrible job of trying not to cry.

And you've been perfect parents.

I'm the furthest thing from perfect. But I'm trying my hardest.

Me too. But . . . I want to keep on having fun. And I might mess up sometimes.

Do you think you can do it without ending up in the hospital?

I'll do my best,

said Darby.

Ben could tell he was smiling.

"Then I guess we have a deal," said Darby's dad. And somehow Ben knew that he was smiling, too.

There were sounds like people doing an excellent job of hugging and blowing their noses and wiping the tears off their faces, followed by the sounds of people settling back into squeaky plastic hospital chairs. At which point Ben thought it was probably safe to turn back around.

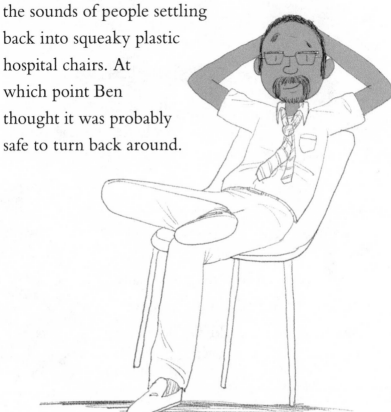

Darby's dad seemed different now, like a more perfect version of whoever he'd been a few minutes before.

Here's a marker,

said Darby's mom.

Who wants to sign the cast?

I do!

said Janet.

Me too,

said Ben, who was ready for the question.

He reached into his pocket and pulled out the gold metallic paint pen he'd used to gild the helmet of his Ben-Hur costume the previous Halloween.

I brought my own.

Darby's parents went
to get some coffee, and
Ben and Janet got to work.
Janet wrote *Janet is great*.

Ben drew a crooked
golden line that snaked
up one side of Darby's
cast and down the other.

"What are you doing?" asked Darby.

"It's called kintsugi. It's when you stick
broken pottery back together with gold so you
never forget that it used to be broken."

Ben added a new line that branched off
from the first, and then a third one that branched
off from that. Slowly a web of golden veins began
to appear.

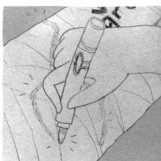

Darby smiled back. "According to the doctors, I'll have six whole weeks to think about how imperfect I am."

"Imagine how much more calculus you'll be able to learn," said Ben.

"Yes. I'm excited!" said Darby. "But the second this cast comes off, I'm gonna try other things, too."

"Like what?" Ben asked.

"Oh man," said Darby, "I don't know. *Everything.*"

asked Janet.

"Then definitely archery. Being imperfect really opens up the possibilities."

"So you're done with perfection?" Janet asked.

"Oh, I'll still try to be as perfect as I can," said Darby. "But I'll also try to be okay with it whenever I'm not."

"What *else* do you want to try?" asked Ben.

"I don't know. Soap carving. Competitive dog grooming. Maybe even baseball."

Ben was surprised. "But it's *literally* impossible to be perfect at baseball."

"Strangely, I'm okay with that," said Darby. "I know *you* don't love baseball, but what if it turns out *I* do?"

At that moment, the part of Ben that loved baseball stood up and grabbed a megaphone.

ACTUALLY, I DO LOVE BASEBALL.

Darby seemed confused. "But you told me that—"

"I really, *really* love baseball." Ben needed Darby to hear just how much.

"Then . . . you should play it."

Darby's words were like a traffic light that has been stuck on red forever and suddenly switches to green.

"Even if I know I'll never be able to do it perfectly?"

"*Especially* if you can't."

Did you hit your leg on Dead Man's Tree, or was it your head?

asked Janet with a look of joyful befuddlement.

She had a point. Darby was the opposite of himself. It was hard to get used to.

"I hit everything at once," said Darby. "The Chute taught me how to look at things differently."

Ben understood. The Chute had strong opinions. It had taught him how to play piano. And just now it had reminded him how much he loved baseball.

Suddenly all Ben wanted to do was swing a bat.

His heart leaped.

"What day is it?"

"Friday," said Janet.

"What *time* is it?"

"Four-thirteen," said Darby.

"Oh boy," said Janet. She knew what Ben was thinking. It was game day. "Can we still make it?"

"It depends how fast your mom can drive."

"Then we can *definitely* make it," she said with the kind of grin some people might find worrisome.

Ben looked over at Darby. He felt bad that they were already leaving. "I'm sorry, but—"

"Go," said Darby with a smile.

"Are you sure that—?"

"GO!" said Darby. "Go play baseball. Go have fun. And then come back and tell me all about it."

Ben smiled and went skipping out the door, ready to play baseball, knowing he'd never be perfect, and feeling in his gut that pretty darn good was more than enough.

CHAPTER 29

It was the bottom of the fifth inning when they got to the school. Ben ran over to the baseball field. His team was playing the Land Sharks, who tended to hit a lot of ground balls. Strong fielders like Ben were especially helpful against a team like that.

The Woodchucks were batting. Coach Stout was on the bench.

Hi, Coach, said Ben.

Coach Stout didn't even turn to look at Ben. He stared straight out at the field. He spat on the ground.

I thought you were done with baseball, Yokoyama.

"That was a temporary thing. I just needed to remember how much I love it. Can I play?"

"Our lineup is set."

"Ben can take *my* spot," said Walter. "I like watching better, actually."

"Thank you, Walter!" Ben's heart soared. There was still a chance he'd get to play.

"Where's your uniform, Yokoyama?" Coach Stout spoke like a bored robot watching a movie about other bored robots. "You can't play without a uniform."

Ben can borrow *my* jersey,

said Walter.

It's not even sweaty.

Ben felt guilty for thinking that Walter needed improvement. He was already as pretty darn good as it got.

"Thanks, Walter," said Ben. "You sure you don't mind?"

"The main reason I signed up for baseball was to spend more time with you. I'm just glad you're back. Plus, we're only trailing five to four. If you play, we might actually win!"

Ben was excited! Their games were almost never that close.

"So, Coach . . . can I play?"

Coach Stout still wasn't looking at Ben. "We really could have used you in the third."

"I'm sorry about that. But I'm here now."

"Tell me why I should let you play."

Ben thought about telling Coach Stout he'd rediscovered his love of baseball while risking his life to save a friend but opted for the simpler approach instead.

"Because . . . the Land Sharks hit a lot of ground balls?"

Coach Stout made the kind of snort that's also a laugh. "That they do. Luckily for you, I really want to win this game, Yokoyama."

"Does that mean I can play?"

"Show me that you mean it. Show me how much you love baseball."

I love baseball,

said Ben.

I don't buy it.

Ben stood up on the bench. "I love baseball!" he shouted. "I love it!"

"I'm still not convinced. Give it some backbone. Show me that you mean it."

Ben dug down to somewhere in the middle of his kidneys and shouted, "I love baseball!" It was the pebble that unleashed the avalanche. "I LOVE BASEBALL!" he sang, walking along the bench, dancing and kicking and waving his arms.

Everyone in the bleachers was staring. Coach Stout was as red as an eight-hour sunburn.

"Get down off the bench, Yokoyama."

"Can I play?"

"You can play. Just stop shouting and get down."

Ben got down. But he kept on shouting on the inside.

When the sixth inning started, Ben went in to play right field. The first batter walked. Then Ben snagged a line drive and threw it to Kyle at first for a double play. Ben caught a pop fly to end the inning.

Ben loved fielding.
Ben loved baseball.
Ben was feeling good.

Then it was the bottom of the sixth. Kyle led off with a hit. Then Dougie struck out. Then DJ walked. Then Randy hit a pop fly.

There were two outs. There were runners on first and second. Ben was up to bat. The game was in his hands.

Kyle was fast. If Ben got a hit, his team would probably tie. If he hit a double, his team might even *win*.

Ben had never hit a double.

Don't think about hitting a double,

said Coach Stout.

All we need is a hit. One run at a time.

GO, BEN!

It was Janet. He was so glad she was there.

Go, Benny!

It was Aunt Nora. *And she was eating a banana!*

Ben waved to them all and walked to the plate.

He looked out at the field, where the Land Sharks were carefully positioned, ready to catch or scoop up whatever Ben might send their way. It wasn't just that he had to hit the ball. He had to hit it *perfectly*.

According to his average, there was a 20 percent chance that he'd pull it off. Ben didn't like those odds.

"Remember what I told you about hitting, Yokoyama."

Ben remembered. Don't *think*. Just *feel*.

Ben suddenly realized! It was the same advice Mrs. Ezra had given him for playing "Clair de lune"!

Coach Stout had said it a hundred times at least. But Ben had never understood what it meant until just now. He wondered if it was possible to play piano and baseball at the same time.

Ben told his brain to go stand in the corner and think about calculus. Then he closed his eyes and turned to his heart.

AWW MAN!

As his fingers gripped the bat, they tapped
out a melody and made the shapes of chords. Out
flowed "Clair de lune" like it was rising from
behind a mountain at midnight.

Ben let his bat dance to the swing and flow of the music. Everything else faded away. He was *ready*. He was—

"Why aren't you pitching, son?" It was the umpire, shouting out toward the pitcher's mound.

That kid has his eyes closed,

the pitcher replied.

I don't want to hit him with the ball.

What are you doing, Yokoyama?

Coach Stout demanded.

Open your eyes.

But Ben wasn't ready. Not *yet*. He let the music flow up from his toes, pulsing through his kneecaps, tracing the swirl of his stomach, and exploring his elbows and wrists before gushing out like a symphony through the tips of his trembling fingers. He let it go anywhere it wanted. *Except* inside his head.

"His eyes are still closed," the pitcher shouted. "I think there's something wrong with him."

"That's it, Yokoyama!" growled Coach Stout. "Get back to the bench."

Just then, the song ended. Ben opened his eyes. He was as ready as he was ever going to be.

I'm okay!

he said.

Go ahead and pitch.

Coach Stout grunted and shook his head.

The pitcher gave Ben a puzzled look. He wound up and threw the ball.

Ben let it slide past. He heard it smack into the catcher's mitt.

STRIKE ONE

said the umpire.

Kyle gave Ben a look that said, *Please don't mess this up.*

"You can do it, Ben!" Janet shouted.

Ben's brain said nothing. It was busy thinking about calculus.

The pitcher threw the ball. Again, Ben watched it go sailing by.

STRIKE TWO!

"What are you thinking?" screamed Kyle. But Ben still wasn't thinking at all.

"Hit the ball, Ben!" said Janet.

"Come on, Yokoyama!" said Coach Stout.

Are you sure you don't want my help?

asked Ben's brain.

I'm sure,

said Ben's heart.

Go *AWAY.*

The pitcher threw the ball.

I've got this,

said Ben's heart.

Just leave it to me.

At the exact right moment, Ben swung. He swung with joy, with belief, with the light of the moon.

He heard a crack as the bat hit the ball, which soared high through the air above the field.

The outfielders ran toward the place where they hoped it would land.

Would they catch it, or would it sail past the reach of their gloves? Or would it fly over the fence?

Or might it just keep going,
beyond the edge of the schoolyard,
rising high above the neighborhoods
and into the wide-open sky?

Ben had hit the ball as well as he could.
Which was all he could possibly do.
Where it landed didn't really matter.

317

ABOUT THE AUTHOR AND ILLUSTRATOR

Hello, folks! My name is Matthew, and I wrote this book.

Hi! I'm Robbi, and I just got up from a good, long nap.

Matthew: *And . . .* more to the point . . . you *illustrated* this book.

Robbi: Did I? Everything that happened prior to the nap is a meaningless blur.

M: I have a confession to make. It's shocking, and it's going to make you sad.

R: Go ahead and tell me. I'm feeling sturdy.

M: I'm glad you're taking this so well. But I'm not quite finished. I also have to admit that . . . this *book* isn't perfect. In fact, I've never written a perfect book and never will. No matter how good a book might be, there's always *something* I could do to make it even better. But if I kept working on it forever, people would never get to read it. Eventually, I decided it was pretty darn good enough, and *that's* when I knew I was done.

R: That was a beautiful speech, Matthew.

M: I'm surprised you're not more emotional.

R: I'm weeping on the inside.

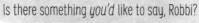

Is there something *you'd* like to say, Robbi?

I want some soup.

I thought maybe you'd like to admit that . . . *you're* not perfect, either?

You can't prove it.

. . .

Your shirt is inside out.

I'm doing it as a favor for the marketing team. But while we're at it, if anyone wants to write us an email, check out our other books, or ask us to come visit their school, library, or conference, they should go to

robbiandmatthew.com

Or they can find us on YouTube or Instagram.

YouTube
Robbi & Matthew

Instagram
@robbi.and.matthew

You're not the only shameless one, Matthew!

M: So long, folks!

R: This is the part where Matthew goes off to write a book and I go buy a camera for no particular reason.

M: But first, let's have some soup.

R: Actually, I kind of feel like making pancakes. If only I had a really good recipe . . .

HOW TO MAKE A
PERFECT*
PAN CAKE
(AND NOT A SMOLDERING WAFER OF CHARBROILED MISERY)
IN 19 SIMPLE STEPS
* AS YOU ALREADY KNOW, THIS IS IMPOSSIBLE

GETTING READY

1) Find the stove.

HINT: It's bigger than the toaster and smaller than the fridge.
It's roughly cube-shaped and is almost certainly in the kitchen.

(SMALL)

(HINT: IT'S THIS ONE)

(LARGE)

2) Find an adult to be your assistant. Stovetops are treacherous!

BRING IT.

3) Cultivate a positive-yet-realistic attitude by saying these things:

I *can* make pancakes.

My pancakes probably won't be *perfect*.

My pancakes might be *prett* darn good!

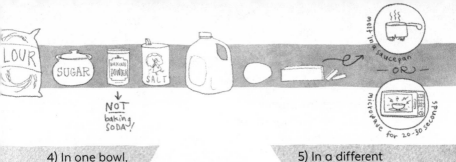

LOUR

SUGAR

BAKING POWDER

↓
NOT
baking
SODA!

SALT

melt in a saucepan
— OR —

microwave for 20-30 seconds

4) In one bowl, mix the dry ingredients:

MIXING

5) In a different bowl, mix the wet ingredients:

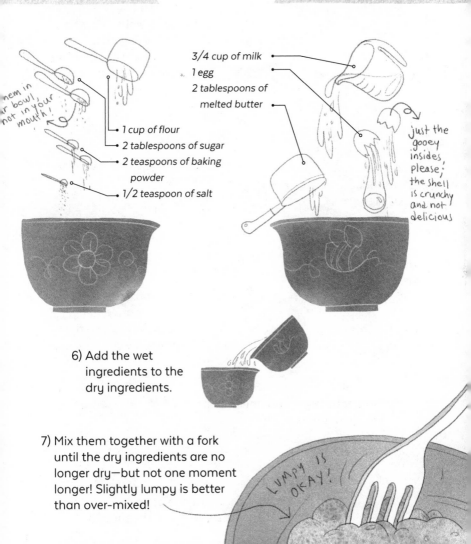

3/4 cup of milk
1 egg
2 tablespoons of melted butter

em in
r bowl,
not in your
mouth!

1 cup of flour
2 tablespoons of sugar
2 teaspoons of baking powder
1/2 teaspoon of salt

just the gooey insides, please; the shell is crunchy and not delicious

6) Add the wet ingredients to the dry ingredients.

7) Mix them together with a fork until the dry ingredients are no longer dry—but not one moment longer! Slightly lumpy is better than over-mixed!

LUMPY IS OKAY!

COOKING

8) Turn one of the burners to medium heat. Place the nonstick skillet on the burner. Add a pat of butter for maximum delight.

9) Using a 1/4-cup measure, scoop blobs of batter into the buttery skillet, leaving space between blobs for blob expansion.

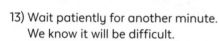

10) Wait patiently but attentively while your pancakes cook.

11) Do not choose this moment to fix that flat tire on your bike.

12) When the batter starts to bubble in the middle, use a spatula to flip each pancake so the other side can cook.

13) Wait patiently for another minute. We know it will be difficult.

14) Remove the pancakes from the skillet with the spatula.

ENJOYING

15) Put your pancakes on a plate, admire them intensely, and gloat a little, knowing you're a better cook than Ben's mom.

16) Don't gloat so long that your pancakes get cold.

17) For extra excitement, add maple syrup, yogurt, honey, dried apricots, blueberries, chocolate chips, and/or chopped pecans (which will be even tastier if your adult assistant can help you toast them).

18) Eat and enjoy as your soul rejoices and your stomach thanks you.

19) If your pancakes were a total disaster, go back to step one and try again. Practice might not make perfect, but it should eventually result in pancakes that are pretty darn good—and maybe even pretty darn great.

Author-illustrator and husband-wife duo
Matthew Swanson and **Robbi Behr** are
co-creators of the critically acclaimed mystery
series the Real McCoys and the picture books
Sunrise Summer, Babies Ruin Everything, and
Everywhere, Wonder—in addition to sixty or so
self-published books for children and adults.
They spend their summers running a commercial
salmon-fishing operation on the Alaskan tundra
and the rest of the year making books, visiting
schools, speaking at conferences, and living in
the hayloft of an old barn on the Eastern Shore
of Maryland with their four kids and one small
dog named Dumbles.

robbiandmatthew.com